Aquarius

Murders of the Zodiac Book 1

Paris Morgan

Contents

To my hubby: Always patient, willing to let me follow my passions and dreams. Thank you, honey.

Chapter 1

Leslie Boxe

My first call was of a possible homicide at a location in a central Dallas neighborhood. It was my first day as a detective, and I hadn't even checked in with my new partner, Joe Roland.

Finding his desk empty, I made my way to the desk sergeant to see what I was supposed to do.

"Has Detective Roland headed to the scene of the homicide?" I felt like the new kid at school. I didn't want to leave if I was supposed to ride with him.

"No, he radioed in for you to meet him there." He didn't even look up to see who he was talking to, but continued to work on his crossword puzzle.

"Can you let Detective Roland know I'm heading over there now?"

"Why don't you tell him yourself when you get there. Or, better yet, use your radio or phone to communicate. I'm not a secretary." He lifted his head to glare at me.

"Yes, sir." I fled to the parking garage where my car was, since I hadn't been issued a vehicle yet, and that was okay. I preferred to take my vehicle rather than ride in Detective Roland's, as he had a reputation for being trashy.

Once there, I had to park down the street because it was lined with an ambulance, two cop cars, and the coroner's van.

Detective Roland had just pulled up at the other end of the police tape. He was close to retirement, but his slightly overweight frame still held authority. I watched him as he balanced a phone between his ear and shoulder with one hand and a cup of coffee in the other while attempting to close the car door.

Hanging up his phone as he walked up the sidewalk, he asked, "What do we have, Detective Boxe?"

"I just arrived. Who's taking point?"

"You are. I want to see what you're made of."

After we both greeted the officer standing at the door, I took out the gloves I had stuffed in my pocket earlier and pulled them on. Upon entering the home, we found the body only a few feet inside the doorway.

The young woman was lying face down with her arms out, as if to catch her fall. As I had expected, there was blunt force trauma to her head. Taking a moment, I studied her surroundings.

"Well, what do you think, Detective?"

"There doesn't seem to be a struggle. Or, at least, not a very big one. I think she met the person at the door and went to answer the phone. When she turned, with her back to the door, they hit her on the head." I knew he was going to be my training officer for a while, but I had to give him all of my impressions. Not just the facts, but what I was seeing and feeling as well.

"This is a bold killer," I added.

"Hmm. Why would you think that?" He shifted his weight from one foot to the other.

Bending down, I pointed to the cell phone just under the coffee table.

"If he hit her on the head from behind while she was distracted, but not from the front, then she may have trusted him. Why would she let the killer in though?" Detective Roland only rephrased what I'd said.

"I think it was her birthday. Look at the calendar, it's circled and starred. There are fresh flowers on the coffee table. The paper on the couch is open to today's horoscope, but on the floor, just under the victim's hand, is a card with the sign of Aquarius."

"Not bad for your first day. Now, tell me what you missed."

I knew he was simply getting me to do all of the hard work, but Joe Roland was a well-respected cop, so I didn't mind.

"Nothing seems to be stolen. The TV and computer are still here. I'm guessing the primary goal was to kill her, but there doesn't seem to be a reason that stands out right away. I'm sure if we wait for the autopsy report, they can tell us what kind of weapon was used."

"Don't give me that line. It's your job to look at this from all angles, and there isn't time to wait for reports. The killer is getting away and your crime scene is getting cold. Forget everything they told you about only looking at the facts. The facts will get you halfway there and help lead you in the right direction, but sometimes you have to trust your instincts and see with something beyond what the facts tell you," Joe instructed me. "Close your eyes and tell me what you see from memory that you didn't mention."

"She was comfortable at home and expecting company, or a delivery." My eyes flew open. "This happened last night. Her birthday was yesterday. Who called in the body?"

Joe let a flicker of a smile flash across his face. "When she didn't show up for work this morning, her boss came to check on her."

"Her boss? Isn't that a little beneath a boss's job description?" I questioned with a lifted brow.

"Some bosses care about their employees, and evidently, this girl was more like a part of the family. Why don't you ask him yourself?" Joe pointed to the house next door, where an older man in a suit was sitting on the steps with his head in his hands.

Not sure if this was some kind of test, I went over to get his statement. As detectives, we didn't have body cams, but they gave us recorders if we wanted or needed to use them.

"Hello, sir. Is it okay if I ask you some questions?" I took a seat on the step next to him.

"What?" He looked around frantically and finally settled on my face. "Sure. Might as well get this over with." He wiped at his face to remove the tears streaming down his cheeks.

"How long have you known the victim?" I asked gently, knowing that finding someone dead was a shock, especially when it was a person that you knew.

"Susan Bacon. She started working for me three years ago, just after she got out of college. I thought that someone with a business sense was a good bet, but she taught me so much more than that. She moved my company into the twenty-first century. She was more like a daughter to me than an assistant."

"So there were no romantic entanglements or problems between you and Susan?"

"Of course not. She was half my age, and that would have just been wrong. I'm happily married, and she was in the process of finding someone worthy of her talents. She's been to my home and had meals with my family. There was no illicit affair. Her family was from Oklahoma, and there wasn't a reason for her to return there after school. She applied to my company because I was looking to expand in a few areas and would need someone flexible to go on trips to do business in my stead."

"Can you tell me why you were at her house this early in the morning?"

"Yes, of course. I'd told her last night that I would pick her up on my way to the office so that she would have time to go over the notes with me before our big meeting today. I'm still not used to all these technological terms, or how to work things that change every week. Anyway, I'd called her from the car as my driver got close to confirm that she was ready, but there was no answer. That's completely unlike Susan. She's always on time or early. I've told her she'll never be able to have a life outside of work if she kept it up."

"You encouraged her to participate in things not related to work? Does she have any enemies, or is there anyone that would want to kill her?"

"Susan? No, she could be a tiger when it came to business stuff, but she was just a shy girl trying to make it in the big city. There weren't many friends that she kept in touch with, but no one disliked her. She was always the mediator at work, and helped to contain volatile situations that could get out of hand. We don't have any business-related issues, or people harassing us either. Is it okay if I call my wife?"

"I think that's all for now. Did you give the officer your contact information?"

"Yes, I did, and here's my business card. Anything you need, Detective. But please, find out what happened to her."

"I'm going to talk to your driver for just a second, and then he can take you home or to work."

Joe stood there with his arms crossed, waiting for me to finish.

"Did I miss anything this time?" I inquired.

"Not at the moment. I do want to look at the crime scene again and make sure that the techs did their job."

I held up the crime scene tape that was keeping people off the property for Joe to walk under and then followed him back inside.

The coroner had moved the body, but the blood from the victim's head was still in a pool just inside the doorway.

Stepping over it and into the living room, I went to her bedroom because I wanted a look around her more personal space.

Everything looked normal and was fairly neat for a young woman living on her own. I pulled open the dresser drawers and found all the clothes folded and arranged according to when you would wear them. Her room gave off the impression that she mostly worked, and there was very little downtime.

Other than a few casual clothes, the majority of her closet was filled with business suits and dress shoes.

"Nothing appears to be out of the ordinary or disturbed. I don't think the killer even came into the house. I think he just stood at the door, hit her over the head, and then left," I called out to Joe as I checked the bathroom.

"The officers interviewed the neighbors, but nobody saw anything suspicious last night. This Susan lady kept to herself and didn't bother anyone. What would you suggest we do next?"

"I think it might be a good idea to go to the office and get the closest traffic signal cameras for around the time of the murder and see where those cars lead us."

"Well, that wouldn't have been my first thought, but it works. I'll meet you there."

"Okay." I headed back to my car, checking my phone.

There were five new messages, all from this new dating site I was trying at the request of my friends. I'd hated the idea, but after seeing how Susan hadn't had a life outside of her work, maybe my friends were right. It couldn't hurt to give this dating thing a try and see what came of it.

The Killer

While the police were chasing their tails, I was waiting for my next victim to wake up so that I could bring her flowers for her special day.

Finally, at 10 a.m., she opened the blinds and appeared to be up for the day. Go time.

I went around to the back of the vehicle and opened the doors to retrieve the flower arrangement. The side of my van had a fictitious name of a flower delivery company that would throw the police off for a while.

It was a great vehicle for surveillance. I could change the logos and plates to fit my needs for the day.

I pulled my cap low to cover my face and walked up the neatly groomed yard to ring the doorbell.

It took two tries before she answered the door in her bathrobe, wet hair dripping as she tried to wrap it with a towel.

"Yes, may I help you?" she asked briskly.

"I have a delivery for you. It's your birthday today, right?" I held the vase of orchids out to her.

"Uh, how did you know that?" she questioned suspiciously.

"The florist mentioned it when I picked up the delivery. Also, the balloon on here says 'Happy Birthday'."

She slapped a hand to her forehead. "Of course. I'm sorry. I haven't had my cup of coffee yet."

"Right. Do you mind taking these so that I can get your signature, please?" I pushed the flowers toward her, and she responded as I'd expected.

As she turned back from placing them on the entry table, I gripped the wood tightly and let loose with the other end, hitting her squarely in the head.

The towel that she'd placed over her hair softened the blow, only slightly wounding her. I had to pull back, slinging flecks of blood on the ceiling as I prepared to strike again.

Dazed, she looked at me, not understanding what had happened. I leaned forward and grabbed the top of the towel from her head. With more force than before, I landed it squarely between her eyes, causing her to fall backward, hitting her neck at an awkward angle.

This second blow should have killed her, but I waited until I was certain that it had done its job.

She didn't move, but her body spasmed as a final breath left her, leaving her still and motionless.

I used the towel from her head to wipe the blood from my weapon. I would need it again, and I didn't want to have dried blood incriminating me before I was finished with the job I had to do.

"Thank you, and I hope you have a happy birthday." I quietly closed the door and walked back to the van, my job done for the moment.

Leslie

I walked back into the main area that was reserved for detectives and received snickers from those seated around Joe.

There wasn't an assigned place for me yet, but I wasn't about to let that bother me. I was the rookie all over again now that I was a detective. Things had changed over the years, and while there were many women in the department, those that made it up from patrol officers weren't made from fragile stuff.

Acting like I hadn't heard anything, I pulled up a chair and slung my backpack with my laptop inside, up on the table. Trying to get anything issued from the cost-conscious watchdog was horrible. I was certain that the lady whose job it was to provide me with police-issued equipment was to make my life miserable, so instead, I had a work-only laptop that I'd purchased.

Knocking the feet propped up on the desk next to me to the floor, I opened the computer up and typed in my personal codes to gain access to the network. I typed up a request to the IT department for access to the cameras. It might take a few days, and I would need to butter them up if I was going to get anything done quickly, so I would take the request to them in person once I was finished.

I filled out a report and added my observations and thoughts of the body.

A ding on my phone interrupted me. It was another dating app I'd installed last night while trying to calm my nerves.

The handsome face that popped up couldn't be ignored, and while I had a lot of messages, this showed a ninety-eight percent match.

Suppressing a sigh that would give the guys around me more excuses to tease me, I responded quickly to get his face off of my screen.

"Would you like to meet for coffee?" I typed into the app. It promised anonymity, and the other person couldn't get your information unless you gave it to them.

Before I could close the app and get back to my report, it dinged again with an answer.

"Sure. Where and when?"

The words stared back at me. I was about to set up a coffee date with a complete stranger.

"Seven...at The Donut Shop on Harry Hines."

My finger hovered over the send button just as Joe rapped his knuckles against the desk, startling me.

"Hey, are you done with the report yet?"

"Yeah. I was about to hit sent on the request for IT to check those cameras."

"Well, hurry it up. We've got another body."

"What? I didn't..." I trailed off as I looked at my phone.

A message had come through from dispatch, and I'd pressed send when he'd startled me. I cleared the phone's screen and pushed print.

"I'm driving this time," Joe informed me as I shoved the laptop back into my bag.

"You're the one in charge," I acknowledged, grabbing the request off the printer as we passed. I'd hand-deliver it if by some miracle they didn't get my email request done by the morning.

• • • ● ● ● • ● ● • •

Joe drove to the scene without using the lights, and the message hadn't indicated anything specific except we had another possible homicide.

"Is there something I'm missing here, Joe?"

"No. Why?"

"We already have one dead body assigned to us, and we haven't even gotten a list of possible suspects yet. Why didn't they send this to one of the other teams?" I braced against the dashboard as he turned a corner on two wheels.

"This one appears to be another home entry with no explanation of why. Same M.O. as this morning, even though they were twelve hours apart. It's only two neighborhoods apart, and they could be connected, but we won't know until we check it out." Joe grinned. "And unlike television, we could have any number of cases on any given day. Just because someone dies, doesn't mean that we drop everything and only work on their case. We don't have an hour to do a month's worth of footwork like they do. Although we don't normally have two murders before lunch."

"I'm well aware of the many other cases that come up during a shift. I've worked them from the patrol side, remember?" I wasn't going to take a lot of crap from my partner. Just because I was new didn't mean I hadn't been trained.

He frowned. "Hey, I didn't mean anything by it. This isn't normal, but it does happen. We could go the rest of the week and not have another murder. We get called to anything where death is involved, such as suicides, suspicious deaths, even the elderly when they pass to verify there was nothing out of the ordinary."

"Sorry. I think my nerves have gotten the best of me." I took the olive branch he'd offered.

"It's normal. You didn't flinch this morning, and you saw a few things that other newbies would have missed. Now, let's see how you do on this one." Joe parked with a screech of tires, alerting everyone to the fact that we were there.

Chapter 2

Leslie

The crime scene was similar to the one from this morning. A middle-class neighborhood that didn't see a lot of crime regularly. The front door was open, and I could see the body lying in the entryway. ***

"Seems to be the same type of crime," I commented, snapping on a pair of gloves as I approached just behind Joe.

Blood had never been a problem for me, unlike my mother, who would almost pass out whenever we would need a tooth pulled or required stitches. My sister, Karen, and I hadn't found it to be a problem in our line of work, and it was something that you grew used to when working with the worst kinds of scenes.

The patrol officer kept his back to the door as he began informing us about what had brought us here.

"We got the call about twenty minutes ago. Her brother was going to surprise her by taking her out to lunch for her birthday. He called when he got here, but she didn't answer.

As he knocked on the door, it opened, revealing her body. The paramedics got here first and pronounced her dead. The blood's fresh, so it couldn't have happened more than an hour ago, two at the most."

"Where's he at?" Joe asked him.

"We took him to sit on the back patio and out of the way. We advised him not to call anyone until he'd talked to you." The officer pointed to the side of the house, where a path led to the back.

It felt different to be on this side of a crime scene, where people I'd worked with just a few days ago were treating me like I was the boss. Normally, I'd have joked around about the events to keep things light. This detective gig was going to take some getting used to.

Making my way around the house, I find him where he was told to go. "We understand that you're the one who found your sister?" I questioned.

It was always better to start out with a gentle approach, and I just automatically took the lead. If Joe had a problem with it, he didn't say anything in front of the witness.

"Yes. I was going to surprise her since she worked from home by going out to lunch. Nothing fancy, just a chance to get out and away from things to celebrate her age." He looked up with tears in his eyes. "She was my older sister, and I always teased her about how old she was. It was kind of our tradition."

"You were coming to take her to lunch?" Joe asked, flipping open a small notepad.

"Not exactly. See, she was up all night working, and doesn't get up until at least ten or eleven most days. I was going to surprise her by going out to breakfast. When I called, she didn't answer, and I assumed she was in the shower or something, so I went up to ring the bell. I knew she was up because she opens the front blinds when she's up for the day. The door wasn't quite latched, and when I pushed on it...she was lying there, bleeding."

"Did you touch her or move anything?"

"I was afraid to. It looked like her brains had leaked onto the floor. I almost threw up, but pulled myself together and called 9-1-1. I'm such an idiot. I could have done something."

"No, you did the right thing. She was already gone, and now we can try to find her killer. I'm sorry for your loss. Do you need to call your family?"

"Oh, God," he groaned, putting his head in his hands. "My parents are going to be devastated."

"We're sorry for your loss...and thank you. If we have any more questions, we'll be in contact."

The patrol officer had gone through the house and opened the back door so that we could go straight inside.

"Anything strike you as odd about these two cases?" Joe asked.

"It was their birthday. He or she has watched them enough to know their routines, and that it was a special day."

"Exactly. But there's no real reason that stands out as to why they were murdered. This is the fun part, kiddo. Finding out the why behind it."

I didn't take his calling me kiddo personally, since he was almost old enough to be my father.

We approached the front door, and the body, from a different angle.

I tilted my head, then walked around the circle of the house to come in from the living room to the entry.

"She opened the door to someone that should have been trusted. The flowers look fresh, and I think she had the towel on her head." I pointed to where it had been dropped just inside the door, but a little way from the body.

"I think the person delivered the flowers, and after she took them, she turned, and they hit her over the head like the first victim. Only with the towel up on her head, it wouldn't have caused as much damage, so they had to take a second swing." She pointed to the ceiling, where there were splatters of blood.

"When the killer pulled back, it would have made some mess, but if they swung again, then that's where this blood would have come from that hit the mirror. If the end of the object had already connected, it would have had loose blood to fling in more places. Also, this is much worse as far as the trauma. I think they hit much harder the second time to make sure they did the job." I paused, surveying the scene.

"The towel was gone when they swung the second time. They didn't want to take a chance that it was going to stop the blow. Then they wiped the blood off the weapon and dropped it to the side, which is why it doesn't match where her body landed."

Joe remained silent, and I thought I'd gone too far describing what I could see in my mind. I always talked when I got nervous or excited. Combine the two, and I was a blabbering mess.

He took a step back. "This was premeditated, and not an argument or fit of anger. I'm going to say we're dealing with a man at the moment because of the height and swing, but this was planned, almost like a hit."

"The killer didn't show emotion in the fact that he didn't hesitate. If he had only swung the weapon once, then she might have been dazed, but she would have tried to run or fight. But she didn't, so he reacted quickly to the fact that the first hit didn't kill her immediately. I get the impression that he might have stood here for a second to make sure she was dead before calmly cleaning the weapon and closing the door behind him. We need to ask the neighbors if they saw something. He was here a little longer than the other house." I walked back around to join Joe before we combed the house for anything that stood out.

They had moved the body by the time we got back, and I stepped around the pool of blood to look at the flowers.

"There's a card in here." I pulled it out, but the only thing on the card was the sign of Aquarius with the words, 'Happy Birthday'.

Taking it, I walked out the back door to the brother.

"Was your sister into her zodiac sign and horoscopes?" I slid the card onto the table in front of him.

"Not that I know of. I mean, everyone kind of knows what their sign is, but she didn't follow her horoscope or get readings. Honestly, I don't think we've ever discussed it before. I don't have a clue what her sign is." He shrugged helplessly.

"Okay. Did she have a boyfriend or anyone that would want to hurt her?"

"No. She was a medical transcriptionist for a doctor's office. That's why she worked at night, doing their records for the next day. If things were slow, or she wanted some extra spending cash, she would take on some work from the hospital or another doctor. Nothing that would make someone want to kill her."

"She might have seen something about a patient that she wasn't supposed to know about," Joe commented. "We'll need to get the name of the company that she worked through, and the doctor that she coded for."

"They were done by patient numbers, so she didn't have access to anyone's name. We joked about some of the more interesting stuff whenever we got together, but it didn't mean anything because she had no idea whose records she'd imputed that day. They were sent from the company. I don't think they even had her doing the same doctor's records each day for that very reason."

"All right. You've been helpful. We'll check it out, but she didn't have anyone special in her life?" I brought the question back up because he'd ignored or forgotten it.

"She'd date occasionally, but mostly she'd meet someone on the hookup app. It was never a regular thing, just a night here or there. I'm her brother, so other than the occasional reference, we didn't discuss her intimate life."

"Joe, anything I missed?"

He shook his head no, and I took the card from the table because I wanted to do some footwork and see if there was a florist that might have done the delivery earlier in the morning.

"Let's knock on a few doors and see if we can find someone that was home this morning," he suggested. "You take the other side of the street, and I'll get this one."

It was almost noon and starting to get hot in Texas, even for January. The first two houses directly across from the victim were no answers, but the third house was pay dirt.

A stay-at-home mom who kept watch on the neighborhood answered the door.

"May I help you?" She peeked through the chain until I showed her my badge.

"We're checking to see if you saw anything that happened at the house over there this morning?" I pointed to the obvious house of interest.

"Of course I heard the ambulances, which is a little unusual for our quiet street, but I noticed a delivery van over there at about ten. A regular-looking guy got out with flowers, but the van blocked my view of the door. I do hope nothing's terribly wrong." She held up a shaking hand to steady herself against the door.

"Well, your neighbor didn't make it. Her brother found her and called for help, but he was too late." I wanted to let her know a little bit without revealing that she had been murdered.

"What happened?" The neighbor gasped in shock.

"That's what we're trying to figure out, ma'am. We're just trying to get a timeline and see if you noticed anything that can help us determine how she died."

"Did that delivery man kill her?" the woman barked, jumping quickly to a conclusion.

"We know he made his delivery, but we're not sure if she was allergic to it or what happened."

"That's just horrible to get a gift like that, and then to die from it. If I hear anything, I'll be sure to let you know. Do you have a card or something?"

"I don't..." I started to answer, and then remembered I still had my old ones from patrol. "Here, this is my old card, but it still has my name, and someone can put you through to me."

Joe motioned me back to the car, meeting me there himself.

"No point in checking out any of the others. The ones with a good sight line are all gone or at work. My older lady three doors down didn't even know there were rescue vehicles out here until I rang her bell." Joe opened the door to get in.

"Any chance you can drop me at my car before we get lunch? I'd like to check out a few of the local florists and see if they can point me in the direction of who might have delivered here this morning." I tried not to cringe at the floor covered in trash.

"My car's too much for you, huh? No worries, you're not the first partner to want their own vehicle. It's just the only place I can be messy because my wife is all over my ass at home." Joe grinned at my discomfort.

"Yeah, it's a little more than I'm used to, but I'll get used to it. I also want to have the IT guys run any delivery vans that were in the area last night near the other crime scene and this one. It's a shame neighborhoods don't have cameras. A criminal could completely hide by going out three miles away and we'd never know to flag it."

"True, but nobody wants everything they do to be tracked. Even the good guys like a little privacy."

While Joe was driving, I pulled up florists and quickly had a list based on how close the locations were to the crime scenes.

"One of these is just around the corner. Wanna save some time and stop on our way back?" I motioned to the shopping center on our right.

"I'll drop you off and run through that drive-thru chicken place for lunch. What do you want?" He turned into the lot faster than was necessary.

A quick glance at the clock showed it was almost lunchtime. "A snack pack of chicken and a sweet tea."

He dropped me off and swung around, making a beeline for the chicken joint.

Someone with talent nicely decorated with hand-painted roses on the door. A bell rang, bringing the clerk's multi-colored head up from her phone. "May I help you?"

"I'm hoping so." It was my first time to flash my badge as a detective. "I need to see if you had any orders for flower deliveries to this address this morning." There was a pen from the counter and I snatched one of the cards sitting on the counter, ready to write down what she said.

She looked at it, turned to the computer, and began typing. "I don't see anything from us, and there's nothing in the national system for me to link it to, either. Sorry, I couldn't be more helpful."

Seeing all the blank cards that anyone could pick up, I turned on my phone and flipped to the picture of the card that had been in the flowers.

"Do you have anything like this available to send out with your flowers?"

"Oh, that's a wonderful drawing, but we don't have anything like that available. It's all the same stock for anyone that orders online or walks in. Something like this would be done in a smaller shop or someone with connections to an artist."

I pointed to the front door. "Who did the front door?"

Her face flushed. "I did."

"Would you know anyone that could do this kind of work and where they might sell it?"

"Most artists that do drawings like that use tablets now. They could have either drawn it and uploaded it, or done it on the computer. It looks more like it was done on a tablet. The style isn't something that would work on paper as well as in an app. You could change the colors to match whatever words you have over here on the card." Her shyness fell away as she explained the art process.

"Thank you. Could anyone print out cards like this and make them look professional?"

"Oh, absolutely. The things we can do now look just as great as something original. They sell cards online in small amounts, or bulk, for easy printing."

"Great. You've been a big help." I turned to walk away, but had a thought.

"If you hear of or see anything like this again, would you let me know?" I placed one of my cards on the counter.

"Yeah. I just hope you can find whoever you're looking for." She fingered the card between her different colored nails.

Joe was sitting in the car eating when I approached.

"How'd it go?"

"There aren't any deliveries in their system, so it wasn't done online, and could have been a walk-in at any florist shop. Those aren't registered on the national site, so unless we want to visit or call every florist within a twenty-mile radius, we're at a dead end." I took the box he offered. My stomach grumbled as the smell of freshly fried chicken hit my nose.

Silence fell as I stuffed my face with the delicious food. "Do detectives always get to have hot food?"

"More than patrol officers do. You have to learn to disassociate from any crime scene that you're at and eat when it's time," Joe advised around a mouthful of food.

"Oh, I showed her the card that came with the flowers. She said it looked like it was done by an artist rather than just a computer-generated icon. When we finish eating, I'd like to go back to that first scene and see if we can find a card or something like this that we missed that would connect the two scenes." I closed my eyes, the sweet tea hitting the spot.

Joe wiped at his mouth with a paper napkin.

"You know, most cases aren't solved on the first day. You kind of have to pace yourself, or the chief will have you working all the time. But I know how it is the first day with all of that enthusiasm, so I guess we can make a second pass." He started the car, heading back to Susan's house, the first victim.

"Not all murders are connected, either. Serial killers are rare, even though that's what's always shown on TV because they're the most sensational. These two murders are most likely not connected at all. Maybe it's just a coincidence that they were in the same area."

"You're probably right, but I just have a feeling that we missed something on the first one. The fact that they were killed only a day apart on their birthdays is what's bothering me the most."

I collected our trash and put it back in the bag so that I could dispose of it later. Even though it looked like Joe didn't know where any trash cans were located, I wasn't going to keep riding in his car and adding to the problem.

The only thing left from this morning was the crime scene tape. It was eerily quiet inside as we pulled our gloves on and walked over the outlines and into the empty living room.

"I don't see how we could have missed anything." Joe moved around carefully, appraising the scene to see if anything stood out.

"The bedroom!" I exclaimed. Racing back to her room, I started pulling out drawers.

"What are you talking about?" Joe had followed me, but at a much slower pace.

"She has lacy underwear." I held up a pair in my gloved hand like it was evidence.

"What in the world are you blabbering about? Most single women have lacy underpants, don't they?"

"True, but the majority of her drawers are filled with nice stuff. A girl from small-town Oklahoma isn't going to own mostly lacy stuff. She's going to have a few nice pairs for a date, but will wear the comfortable ones unless she's dating regularly." I smiled triumphantly.

"That doesn't mean she was dating. Maybe she just went out occasionally to scratch an itch and then came home. Her boss said she worked all the time and didn't have time for other stuff."

"Well, bosses can be wrong. I need to look through her social media and phone stuff. I'm pretty sure that she had a boyfriend, at least recently. I still want to find that card," I muttered, walking back to the living room.

"I'm so glad that you're here to tell me things I would have missed."

Ignoring him, I continued to look at the room from the kitchen's point of view.

Then I saw it, mixed in with the mail that had dropped when she'd fallen. One of the techs must have put it back on the desk when they were done.

A note card with the sign of Aquarius, with the words 'Happy Birthday' printed, but no signature.

Joe was standing next to me with an evidence bag for the card.

"Good job, kid. Let's call it a day and go back to process this, see if we can find anything on these cards."

Chapter 3

Leslie

My alarm went off an hour and a half before I had to be at work, but that wasn't what had me groaning. It was the coffee date I'd agreed to the day before.

Why did I do things like this to myself? There was no way that a cup of coffee before work was going to be enough to tell me if we would hit it off. Then again, having coffee meant that he wasn't going to expect to get to home base the first time we met.

Standing in front of my closet wasn't helpful, because I was honestly clueless what I should wear. I had to go to work afterward, so I compromised and went with a pair of casual khaki pants and a dress shirt. I was still too new from my patrol beat to feel comfortable in women's dress shoes or heels. My dress boots were hidden, but I didn't have to worry that they would hold up if I had to chase someone.

Hair and makeup didn't take long, and before I knew it, I was parked and in the coffee shop, waiting on a guy who looked like his picture to walk through the door.

My phone dinged, and I was busy looking at the message to see the second he walked in.

He was about six foot two, good-looking, with blond hair and a clean-shaven style. Not my usual type of bad-boy-trying-to-do-good, but maybe I could make an exception in his case. He made a straight line toward me, and I had to tear my eyes away from his physically fit body.

"Hi. I'm hoping you're Leslie?"

"Uh, yeah, and you must be Jerome. It's nice to meet you. Should we get some coffee and something to eat?" I nervously suggested.

"Of course." He stood back so that I could walk in front and order first.

It was now or never, and I needed a real breakfast before I went to work, so I ordered a burrito, orange juice, and to-go coffee. If he couldn't handle my job, it was best to get it over with now.

"You must have worked up an appetite while waiting for me." He gave me a charming grin that threatened to melt the walls I normally kept up.

"Sort of. I need a good meal before I start my shift. It could be a while before I get a chance to eat again." Before I could say anything else, he started to order.

"I'll have a to-go coffee and a banana, please." He pulled out his wallet.

"No, I've got this one." I waved his money away. I'd wanted us to go Dutch, but I decided that paying for all of it was better than being obligated to him if things didn't work out.

"For today. I'll get it next time." He confidently stepped to the side to wait for our order. "So, what do you do for a living that has you skipping meals?"

I took a deep breath. "I'm a police detective."

"Really? That must be fascinating. Getting to catch the bad guys and knowing that you're making the world a better place."

"It can be, if you find the one who committed the crime. I work homicides, so I tend to see the worst in people." I cringed and turned to grab the tray as they called our number.

"I could see how that makes things more difficult. You're always seeing people who've had a bad day, and it's hard to think of rainbows and unicorns after facing death daily," he sympathized.

Staring at him seemed to be a thing, as I gaped at his words. Could I have found someone that understood my job? Time to put some of my skills to use instead of letting him carry the conversation.

"What do you do for a living? It didn't say on your profile."

"Oh, I do articles for a few magazines here in Dallas. I gather all the research and do the outlines of facts for the first draft, then they write it and put their bylines on it."

"That's terrible. Why would you let someone else get the credit for your work?"

He smiled at my offense on his behalf. "I'm just a well-paid fact-checker. Writers don't always have time to do all the research on a subject, but they need to make sure that it's done correctly so they don't get sued. I do the reading and computer search for them so they can publish, knowing they're giving their people the best information on any given topic. I'm kind of the insurance person for writers. It's cute that you would get upset on my behalf, though."

"I'm surprised that I reacted so strongly, but I'm kind of a black and white kind of girl. There isn't much room for the gray or crossing lines in my job, and that just sounds like they're cheating or something." I slapped my hand over my mouth in horror. "I just went way too deep for a coffee date. My bad, I apologize. My mouth is the thing that gets me in the most trouble with people."

"No worries. Any woman that can become a detective has to be tough and opinionated to make it to that type of position. What made you want to be a cop in the first place?" He paused. "See? Now I've done it too, asking a deep question that should be for a later date."

"This is one question I don't mind answering. My sister is a cop, and when she first got started, I thought she was crazy. I mean, who wants a job where they get shot at? Then I started listening to some of the stories where she was able to help people, and I knew when I got out of college that I'd join the academy."

"Now, for on to a lighter subject. Are you a dog or cat person?" He took a sip of his coffee.

"Neither, really. That's why I did the dating app. I don't have much of a life. I'm gone too much to have a pet and still give them the attention that they deserve. Which is one of the reasons that I was reluctant to fill out the profile for a date. I have a hectic schedule, and it doesn't leave much room for relationships."

"Well, I think that any man who meets you could see that your job comes first. That's not necessarily a bad thing. It means that if you ever fall in love, you'll be just as passionate about that person as you are about your job."

I could feel a blush creeping up my cheeks. To hide it, I took a large drink of orange juice, only to choke because I'd drank it too fast.

Jerome reached over and began patting my back. "Whoa, I hope I didn't offend you."

"No, you didn't. I'm just not used to doing this kind of thing." I wiped my chin to make sure that I hadn't dribbled on my shirt or anything.

"The not being in control of everything, or having a conversation with a guy you might be interested in?" Jerome crossed his arms with a smirk.

"Ah, well, you are very interesting. But I'm not a control freak, so I'm not sure how that applies here." I knew as soon as the words left my mouth that he had me figured out. I could never let someone else be in control, and it was one of the reasons that I didn't have lasting relationships.

"How about we compromise? Dinner tonight, but you choose the place so that you feel comfortable, and we can ask light questions that we should have asked this morning?" He glanced at his watch. "I've got a meeting in twenty minutes, and it'll take most of that to get there."

Unable to meet his eyes, I focused on the top button of his shirt. "Yes, to dinner. Just tell me where you want to go. I'm not that picky."

He studied me for a moment before replying. "The Italian place off the Central Expressway at seven."

"Done. I'll be thinking of questions for dinner." I grabbed my coffee and uneaten burrito before I fled the scene.

I arrived at Joe's desk, out of breath, but not for the reason that he assumed.

I had a date tonight, and I had no idea how that had happened. I hadn't chased this guy off yet. Well, there was always tonight for him to run away from me screaming.

• • • ● ● • ● ● • •

"What's the plan for today?" I wanted to get the conversation off of me to help avoid questions.

"A visit to the morgue so we can make sure that these cases are both connected. I know we found cards at each of the crime scenes, but it's always better to collect as many facts as possible. Did you think of anything last night that might help?"

"What makes you think I worked on this last night?" I shoved the last bite of the burrito into my mouth, glad that something good came from my morning stop.

"You're new and eager to prove yourself. Plus, this is one of those cases that if we don't crack it in the next forty-eight hours, it'll become a cold case. Our chances become very slim on finding who did this."

Joe pulled out his keys.

"Nope, I'm driving today." I figured he could wait to find out what I'd discovered on the way to the morgue.

"Oh, great," Joe grumbled, following me. "Taking the lead already."

"Not exactly. I just want to smell like me at the end of the day and not like fried chicken." I stuck my tongue out at him as we walked out to the parking garage.

"So, what did you discover last night?" Joe waited for me to unlock his door.

"I got on all their social media sites last night and looked through their profiles. Susan had her work stuff separate from her private stuff. She had two accounts, so her boss didn't see what she did when she wasn't working. She seemed to be into a less than traditional sex life." I concentrated on bypassing the morning traffic that the freeways were congested with at this time of day.

"You mean, like, a private club?" He shifted uncomfortably.

"Yes, but I found two or three people that might be able to shed light on her more current activities."

"What about our other victim, Heather?"

"Most of her stuff was pretty normal. Since she worked late, there weren't a lot of friends that she did stuff with. She had a few girlfriends that she kept in touch with, but it looked like she was more of a homebody than victim number one." I pulled into the morgue's parking lot and waited for Joe to get out so that I could lock it up.

"Let's see if we can find out what the murder weapon was so that we can run it through the database for similar crimes. This might not be this guy's first try at this."

"Agreed. If it is, he got really lucky on not leaving much evidence behind."

"Anyone that watches TV or does their research can figure out how to avoid leaving a trace. But lucky for us, the majority of criminals aren't that smart." Joe led the way inside since I'd had no idea where we were going.

Joe stopped outside a set of swinging doors and swiped his ID card, which granted us entrance into the room.

"Hey, Caleb," Joe called out to a middle-aged guy removing someone's vital organs.

Even though I wasn't squeamish, seeing something that belonged on the inside of a body hadn't been on my to-do list for today.

"Joe, I see you've brought your new side piece with you." He barely glanced up at us.

"Excuse me?" I frowned. He should know better than to say something like that.

"What?" He looked up at the sound of my voice. "Joe didn't show you his new gun?"

"No, he didn't." I gave Joe a dirty look for not warning me about this guy.

"So, what do you have for us on the two dead bodies?" He stood at the edge of the room, not going any closer to the table than he had to.

"I wrote the reports up last night. Give me just a second to record this, and I'll go over it with you." He put an organ on the scale and made a notation on his tablet. We watched as he bagged it up before pulling his gloves off with a snap.

"We're talking about the two victims of blunt trauma that came in before noon yesterday, correct?"

"Yeah. Do you already have a cause of death?" I had to tread carefully. I didn't want to get on the bad side of anyone this early in my career. These guys were the ones that could make or break a case with their testimony and evidence.

"It was a light day, but we had three gunshot victims last night. I don't have much extra time, so let's get to it." He picked up a file and flipped it open. "This first one was from the day before. She'd been dead at least twelve hours when it was called in to you guys. It was a quick hit to the middle of the forehead, probably when she turned back around. He was able to take her by surprise because there were no signs of struggle. The blow would have knocked her unconscious and fractured her skull, causing her to die rather quickly."

"The second victim, he had to hit twice to accomplish his goal. The first blow simply dazed her, and he had to hit her harder the second time so that she couldn't fight back or call for help. You'll see here in the X-rays that he crushed her skull in, which is why there was tissue leaking out from the wound." He closed the folder and placed it on top of the other one.

"What kind of weapon did he use to do this?" I posed the question when it looked like Joe wasn't going to say anything.

"It was a six to a twelve-inch wooden weapon, like a large handle to something." He demonstrated with his hands.

"Could he have exerted that much force to cause that kind of damage with something less than a foot long?" Joe questioned from behind me.

"I'm going to guess that he was able to swing it in a downward motion, which puts him at a little taller than both women. I'd estimate at least six feet, considering that they were both under 5'6". If he was determined and knew what he was doing, then this would have been fairly easy. I didn't detect any hesitation on the first one, just a good clean blow to the head. The second one received two blows, but from the pictures of the crime scene, it appears that she had a towel on the top of her head. That would have changed the effectiveness and made the second blow a requirement if he was intent on causing her death." He continued to talk as he walked over to the wall and grabbed another pair of gloves. "If you find anything, or come across something that looks like it might have been used, send me a picture and I'll see if I can match it."

"Thanks for your time, Caleb." Joe hurried back out into the hallway. Following him out, he turned to me, exhaled, and took a deep breath. "I hate going in there. Dead bodies are fine until they're cut open, and he's playing around with their insides. I've seen lots of zombie movies, and I always expect it to come alive with its chest open and bite him." He shivered before straightening up. "Anyway, do you have a possible lead on a boyfriend or partner for Susan?"

"Yes, and then I thought we'd take a crack at her boss again. It's hard to imagine that they were close and that he had no idea that she might be seeing someone."

The name I'd found led us to an office complex downtown for an oil company's office.

Noah Preston worked as an executive of the oil portion of the Urban Energy's Natural Department.

"May I help you?" his secretary asked as we stepped through the door to their offices on the tenth floor.

"Yes, we're here to see Noah Preston about a personal matter." I held up my badge for her to look at, then placed it back on the belt of my slacks. At least I'd worn makeup today, so I didn't feel as underdressed when she got up and walked to the conference room with us following her in her four-inch heels that looked expensive and dangerous.

"If you'll wait in here, Mr. Preston will be with you short-ly." She closed the door without even offering us anything to drink.

"Well, she's not the kind of girl that you take home to Momma, but if Susan was any indication of his taste, I'd say he goes for the more power-driven type," Joe commented, taking a seat.

I preferred to stand so that I could pace. It was going to take a while for me to get used to walking less each day. I was going to have to make up for it when I hit the treadmill on my days off.

The door opened, and a handsome man in his thirties walked in and took a seat. "Cassie said that you wanted to see me about a personal matter?"

"Yes. Were you acquainted with Susan Bacon?" Getting right to the point, I settled into the chair across from the one he'd taken.

He looked at me suspiciously. "I was. I would say that we had a mutual relationship. Is she okay? Did something happen?" His calm demeanor changed slightly as he realized that we wouldn't be there if she was okay.

"I'm afraid not. She was murdered in her home, and we've been trying to find someone that knew her outside of work. Were you seeing each other?" Joe leaned forward in the chair, doling out information and watching his reactions closely.

"We weren't dating, but we had the occasional moment of passion. I'm sorry to tell you that I didn't even know where she lived, as we always met at a safe location and never used our homes." He looked upset, but not devastated.

"How did the two of you meet?"

"Um...it was at a club, and mutual friends introduced us. It's a private club, but I could get the name of one of our friends that could verify we only met there." He was being cagy about the facts.

"The Black Tie Club?" I inquired, acting like I was consulting my notes.

He ran a finger around his collar, loosening it nervously. "Y-Yes. It's a private club, and no one is supposed to talk about it...you know, like fight club. And how did you know the name?" he asked accusingly.

"I'm a cop. It's my job to know about all sorts of private things, like exclusive clubs where people might find themselves murdered in their homes after they've seen something or someone they weren't supposed to see." I grinned, watching as he tried to keep his composure.

"Am I being charged with something? Do I need to call my attorney?"

"Not right now. We were just having a friendly meeting to get some additional information about Susan and anything that might have caused someone to want to murder her in her home. If you don't know anything about that, we'll let you get back to your day." Joe got up and held out his hand.

Slipping my card onto the conference room table, I advised, "If you think of anything, or something comes up that makes you change your mind about talking with us, that's my number, and I can be reached anytime."

A guy like Noah would be wondering how much I knew about his kinky lifestyle and might think that I would want to hook up instead of throwing his ass in jail. There was more to this murder than just a simple act of killing, and I was willing to bet that Noah Preston was involved in some way.

Chapter 4

Back at the station, I did a little digging online and pulled up as much information as I could on Noah Preston. They considered him a rising star in his company, Urban Energy, and was on track to be promoted to office manager of his division. There was no mention of his off-hour activities, or that it was something public. Most of the time, clubs like the Black Tie were hush-hush and kept secret. Like most elite clubs, you had to know someone and get a recommendation to be invited inside.

"Crap!" I muttered out loud.

Nick, who was passing by, looked over my shoulder. "Hey, I know a guy that could get you into that club if you wanted to. It's an expensive buy-in for guys, but women normally get in at a lower cost. Couples have the same buy-in as guys do. Someone has to sponsor or mentor you. You can't just go inside without some sort of guide."

I protested that I wasn't interested, but it might be a good way to see what Noah was really into.

"Thanks. Can you send me the information? I think my victim used to go there, and I may need a way inside."

"Uh-huh. Your victim is the reason that you want an invitation, but yeah, I can see if he can get you in." Nick patted my shoulder and kept moving before I could defend myself.

Great. Now all the guys would think that I was willing to accept their jokes and advances. I'd taken all my credibility away with one computer search. At least I knew that Susan had to have been invited to the club, and that someone had to sponsor her. I would have to do this part of my research from home after my date this evening.

I moved onto the next item on my list, which was the murder weapon. A google search revealed a few ideas, including one that seemed a little crazy to me—nun chucks. However, I ran several different searches with the criteria of a wooden object that matched or came close to the description that Caleb Jones, the coroner, had given us.

Printing out a report on possible matches, I was on my way to the printer when Nick stopped me.

"Here's the number of my friend. You have to tell him you're a cop first or he'll be very pissed when he takes you and finds out later. Trust me, you don't want him on your bad side. Anyway, he sometimes takes guests, and you could go and observe for the night. If he takes you, then you won't get into trouble. He'll be responsible for you." He handed me a paper with a simple name of Ford and a number written on it.

"He only goes by this name there. I'm not sure if it's his real name or not. I didn't ask because I sometimes need his help when a case gets a little on the sensual side." Nick lifted an eyebrow. "Don't judge me."

Relief flooded my face at his words. "Thanks for doing me a solid. It will help, even if he can just give me some insight into this other guy we're looking at as a possible suspect."

"No worries. I know you're new, and this is someone that might help, whether it's now or in the future. Hope you can catch this guy." He walked back toward his desk on the other side of the room.

The printer stopped spewing out pages for me and I took them, along with the card from Nick that could help solve the case.

Ten pages of possible matches would take some time to wade through and mark off. I looked around curiously, noticing that my partner had vanished. Knowing he could find me if he needed to, I started poring over the papers. This guy could have been working in the metroplex, and we might not have connected other crimes because the crime scenes weren't the same, or no one had put them together before.

Out of the ones listed, or that had been put in the system properly, there were ten that stood out as possible connections. I marked and looked up each case in the system to see if there had been any arrests in those cases.

Several seemed to fit the weapon used, but they were obvious crimes of passion, or there was a witness to the murders.

Only two fit all of the details, but they were in Ft. Worth's jurisdiction, and I wasn't sure how we did things like that with an intercity connection. Joe would be the one I would need to ask, because some departments were glad for the extra help, and others got seriously pissed off that you were trying to make the collar for your city.

Pulling out my phone to text him a message, I noticed it was already two in the afternoon. No wonder he'd disappeared. I'd missed lunch and would have to see if I could scrounge something up.

"Hey, I might have a lead. I'm heading to grab some lunch across the street over at the food trucks. I'm going to need your help to figure out the next step if you want to meet me out there."

I closed everything up and put it all in my pack before I walked out to find some food.

The food trucks weren't crowded since it was already past the lunch hour, but most of them stayed around because cops wound up eating at all hours.

Minutes later, I sat down at a table that had a pile of newspapers held down with a rock to keep them from blowing off. What caught my attention was the storyline on the paper, "Birthday murderer is here. More details on page ten."

The food was forgotten as I frantically opened it to page ten and started reading.

"This killer is leaving a calling card with the message 'Happy Birthday'. When answering the door, three women who have no connection to each other, except that they were killed on their birthdays, were bludgeoned to death in the entryway of their homes over the past five days."

A tap on my arm brought me around, and I was reaching for my weapon when I realized it was Joe. "You about gave me a heart attack." I placed a hand over my racing heart.

"What were you so intent on that you didn't hear me call your name?" Joe seated his large frame on the bench next to me with his food.

"This." I tapped a still shaky finger on the newspaper in front of us. "This article is from yesterday, and there are five victims of what they are calling the 'Birthday Killer'."

Joe started reading the article while eating his tacos.

I took a few bites while he caught up on the details.

"Well?" I demanded, as he finished the article and took another bite.

"Mmm hmm," he mumbled with his mouth full.

"I think it's the same killer. That's why I texted you to meet me. I'd found two different cases that matched ours in Ft. Worth, probably two of these. I didn't want to call the detective on the case until I'd had a chance to see how we normally handled something like this."

Joe calmly wiped his mouth. "I was at a doctor's appointment when I got your text. I forgot to mention it this morning. Take a deep breath and another bite of your food before it gets cold."

"But this might be the break we were looking for, Joe," I argued, while grudgingly doing what he said.

"It might be, but look at it this way. Our killer just moved cities, and that means they haven't caught him. That's just made our job a lot harder because he knows what he's doing." Seeing the frown on my face, he continued. "We can certainly see about meeting with the detective in charge. Can't hurt, that's for sure. He might have different details that we've missed. Just calm down, and when we finish eating, I'll see if we can get a meeting this afternoon or in the morning."

Hard as it was to be patient, Joe was right. We couldn't do anything right that moment, so I'd just finish my food. Ugh, I hated when someone else was right, but I'd gotten good at hiding it over the years.

"If this is the same killer, then he hasn't missed a day of killing, and might have someone that he's stalking right now. We don't have much time if he's going to keep doing this." I shoved the last two bites into my mouth and washed it down with my drink.

I refrained from slamming my cup down and screaming, "There!" But it was so tempting.

Joe just shook his head, as if he knew what I was thinking. He probably was, having been on the job for years. It wasn't like I wasn't bouncing in my seat with energy.

He pulled out his phone. "Yes, can you transfer me to the person in charge of the birthday killer case? I'm with homicide over here in Dallas." He nodded, then replied, "Sure. My cell phone number is 555-1111. He can call me whenever it's convenient. Thank you."

"Satisfied?" Joe grinned at my impatience. "Oh, I wish I had your energy."

We both got up and threw our trash away. We'd barely made it inside when Joe's phone went off.

"Hi, Ryan. I think we're both chasing the same killer, and I wondered if we could compare notes? If his pattern holds, he's got someone scheduled to die today in our city, so the sooner the better."

Joe hung up and turned to head for the garage instead of our desks. "Well, what are you waiting for? We're driving over to meet him, and if we want to beat the traffic, we'd better get a move on."

I fell into step beside him. "So you've just been playing it cool and letting me get all excited when you knew the clock was ticking?"

"Yep. Figured it wouldn't hurt you to work a little bit of that extra energy out. You planning to drive again?" He paused at the row where I'd parked my car earlier.

"Absolutely. You've had enough fun for the day, old man." I winked as he grunted in reply.

The Fort Worth Homicide Department didn't look that much different from ours. When we signed in and showed our IDs, the detective met us before anyone could escort us back.

"I'm Ryan Fox, the detective in charge of the birthday killings." He held out a hand, firmly gripping mine in his.

A few years older than me, he was about six feet, and kept in shape. There wasn't an ounce of fat that could hide under his dress shirt.

Joe made the introductions as we followed him to an empty office down the hall.

"My partner was doing some research and discovered the link between our cases. We only have two dead at the moment, and if this is the same guy, then we have at least three more that could end up dead. Leslie?" Joe motioned for me to get out our case files, which I had to run to the office for before we left.

It was that moment of 'I'll show you mine, but need to see yours first,' and since we'd called him, it was in our court.

"These are the two cases that we have so far. I noticed one difference, and that is the cards left at the scenes." I pulled out my phone and showed him the picture of the Aquarius sign from the zodiac calendar.

"You're correct. We didn't put that in the paper so that we could weed out false leads. From what we've uncovered, these have all been done on the female victim's birthday, and a card was found at each scene." Ryan sighed as he recounted the facts to us.

"That's the only thing we've found that each woman had in common with the other. They're all employed, mostly single, but there have been a few that were married and the spouse was out of town. He's picked his victims very carefully and knows them well. From what we can tell, he has to have computer skills, because this is information that can only be attained by having access to the victim's private files at a company or online. Now that you have several in Dallas as well, it's almost a certainty that he doesn't work with them. That would be too much drive time between victims to keep an eye on them. Which narrows it down to cameras in their homes, or a team of people that are working together. "

"You have a little more to work with than we do at the moment, but there doesn't seem to be a motive for these killings. Nothing was stolen, their deaths don't benefit anyone specifically, and no one that we have found yet wanted them dead. Is there anything on this from your side?" I tried to stay professional and keep my eyes off his handsome face. It was hard to maintain eye contact when his eyes were a deep green that made his face just as dreamy as the rest of him.

"No, there seems to be no motive. We've interviewed their families and co-workers, but the only thing connecting them is their birthdays. We've put half of our department on this because we were afraid that our body count was going to keep rising, but nothing's happened over the last two days, and we thought this was a onetime spree."

Ryan pushed the stack of files he'd laid on the desk toward us. "You're welcome to look over these and see if anything stands out to you while I do the same. We put the article in the paper hoping it might save some innocent women from dying on their birthday."

"I think that's the most tragic part of this whole thing, is that they were excited about their birthdays, and this killer is taking that away from them."

Death was never easy to deal with, but someone like this was taking pleasure from ending their lives on what should be a happy and fun day.

"Question. Sorry, I've got a lot of those since this is my first set of cases as a detective. Anyway, looking at these pictures from your files, they look almost identical to ours, but I don't think our killer is doing this out of vengeance, or as a way to get off," I rambled nervously.

"Was there a question in there?" Ryan grinned and exchanged a glance with Joe.

"No. I mean, sort of." I frowned. "These are either hits or someone's on a quest, right? It's appearing as if he just delivers something and does the job. There's no going through their homes for souvenirs or assaults after they're dead. He's not even sticking around to watch them die." I blushed as both men looked at me, waiting for me to finish.

"I think she's answering the questions she's asking all by herself. We should just sit here and let her do all the work." Ryan twirled a pen between his fingers.

"That's all I've been doing since she was assigned to me two days ago. If we could get all the newbies to do this much of the work, then we might not have to do more than eat donuts and drink coffee," Joe agreed amicably.

"All right, have fun at my expense, but what do you think? Is it a paid hit or something to simply check off his list?" My eyes kept darting between them to see who was going to answer.

"So impatient, too, but she does have a point. These don't have the feel of paid hits or assassinations. No one has enough money to pay someone for seven kills in the same area, and I doubt they'd want the amount of heat it would bring on any future killings. Unless this was just a practice run. But they're bunched up too closely to make sense for that. It seems like they're going off of some kind of list," Ryan agreed, tapping on the files laid out in front of us.

"What do their deaths accomplish?" I wondered aloud, glancing at all the files.

A knock on the door interrupted my train of thought.

"Excuse me, Detective, but that lady is here again. She says that she has important information for you." The patrol officer bearing the message waited to see if Ryan had an answer.

"Take her to an open interrogation room. Maybe you two will have some insight into what she's telling me." He got up from the desk and held the door open for us.

"This lady is claiming that she's a psychic, and that she's seen who's doing the murders. So far, I don't think she's very credible. For all I know, she could be the one doing it." Ryan straightened his tie and ran a frustrated hand through his hair.

It was such a cute gesture, and my brain veered off when I realized I had a date tonight. A quick glance at my watch showed it was only four-thirty, and we had two and a half hours before I needed to be at the restaurant.

Joe motioned me to the side, and I was thankful for the distraction. "Why don't you go ahead and see if she'll open up to you since you're a woman? If I think of something, I'll text you and you can ask her."

"Really?"

"Yeah. You've done questioning when on patrol. It's not any different when you're a detective. Just trust your gut and watch her for tells that she's lying, or has more information," he advised.

"Thanks." I took a deep breath and opened the door Ryan had disappeared through.

The psychic wasn't what I'd been expecting at all. She was a younger woman, around twenty-five. Dressed in jeans and a T-shirt, the only thing that might have given someone the impression that she was a little different were the multiple bracelets on each of her arms. She was on the smaller side, her brown pixie cut emphasizing her youthfulness as she played with her necklace nervously.

"Hi, I'm Leslie Boxe. I was consulting with Ryan when he got a message that you were here, so he didn't have time to fill me in on what you know about the birthday killer." I held out my hand, and she hesitated just an instant before accepting. Instead of shaking it, she turned it over and traced the lines on the palm of my hand.

"That's interesting," she mumbled as her index finger moved over the lines several times.

Suspicious at the very broad statement, I sat down and let her finish as she fixed me with a hard stare.

"You have a hard road ahead of you. This year you'll meet your true love, but it will only come after many tears and problems that you will come to find peace. Someone will be your opposite and lead you on a long chase, but in the end, you'll prevail against these killers."

"Any idea who they might be?" Ryan laughed.

"You, young man, shouldn't be so flippant with what you don't understand." She turned her intense gaze to him.

"Your future is tied to hers, and if either one of you dies, it will cause a ripple effect that will destroy your entire family. Even now, evil is stalking you because you wish to bring justice to those that need it. Don't underestimate the bond you two will share. It's important to your survival. He wants to play with both of you before he ends you."

"Yeah, see? You've just convinced me that you're in cahoots with the killer. Does he want to play with us? That's not going to get you any favors, threatening officers of the law. Why should I keep you out of jail?" Ryan almost came across the table at her.

"I'm sorry, I missed your name." I placed a hand on Ryan's arm to help restrain him and bring back some civility to the conversation.

"Flora Martin," she whispered.

"Don't let him bully you, Flora. While I believe you feel strongly about this, what you've said does make it seem like you know more about these murders than you're letting on. Is there anything else that the universe has told you that might be able to help us?" I pleaded nicely.

"You both are already working so well together, good cop to his bad cop. I don't listen to the universe, I listen to what everyone tells the universe. This wasn't the gift that I wanted. I was born with it, and I normally hide it because of situations like this. Unlike the normal situations of advising businessmen, or settling a lover's quarrel, this is going to shake the cosmos to their foundations. Someone wants to harm those who are connected to the greater good. They plan to wipe out the good so they can't make the world a better place."

Ryan sank to the chair in disbelief that Flora had opened up to me. "How does anything you've said prove that you're not part of this evil against the cosmos?"

Flora grinned. "All I had to do was listen to the signs. This is the month of the Aquarius. I'm not completely sure about the zodiac symbols and what they mean, but I do know that everywhere I've gone for the past seven days, I've seen some version of the sign right before I believe that a murder was committed. It's not a science in the way you want your forensics to line up, but there aren't as many people out there that follow astrology or dabble with the stars as there used to be.

"When everything around me is pointing to one conclusion, it generally means that it's a significant item. I've had dreams of darkness for the last month, and on the first day of the new sign, a heaviness settled over me when I woke up. It's not something you can shake, no matter how many cleansings you do. My home isn't as dark as the air outside. It hisses against those that have an inner light within because the evil believes that it will win this battle." Flora shook her head as if to clear her thoughts.

"So this is just a feeling that you've been having, and you don't have anything concrete to give to us?" Ryan banged a fist on the table, wanting to demand her to answer.

"No, I'm sorry. Honestly, I'm just a college student. I don't even read palms for a living. I'm not as connected to the world of my blood as most with my gift are. My mother married outside of the blood, and they left the culture before I was born. I've never actually practiced before. Since I went to college, things have gotten more intense, and I've been studying my family's history. I started having visions in class shortly after Christmas break. If I learn of anything that I can help with, I'll call you." She pulled out a blank card and wrote her number on it.

"The energy the two of you create when you're together swirls faster the longer we're here. I've never seen anything like it before. I'm going to call my mom and tell her she has to come clean about her family." Flora stood, signaling that the interview was over.

"Wait." I pulled out one of my cards and handed it to her. "I know that he's still skeptical, but there are many lives at stake, so anything, day or night, please call us."

Ryan jumped up. "Hold on...you can't just leave."

"She needs to find out why things have changed, and she's seeing things now when she wasn't only a short time ago." I nodded for her to go ahead and blocked him from stopping her.

"I know we've just met, but she not only doesn't fit the profile, but she's also too small to have done the crimes. I'm sure that you've already run her, and she had alibis for the times of the murders, didn't she?"

"Yes," he growled, slamming a hand on the glass. "Why am I taking orders from you? This is my station, not yours."

I moved out of the way. "You're welcome to go after her, but it won't change the fact that she's not your killer."

"How can you be certain?" he challenged, standing over me. "Do you believe in all that universe cosmos bullshit?"

"Believe? I'm not sure that's the correct word for it. Let's call it curiosity. The cards that were left at all the scenes had the Aquarius sign. That can't be a coincidence. I think if we do some research, it might lead us in a direction that we wouldn't have pursued before." I crossed my arms, willing to defend my position.

"You know what? You're right, it can't hurt. We're already chasing our tails, and we don't even have a suspect. Let's take the night and see what we can come up with. That might make more sense tomorrow."

Joe stepped in at that point. "You two ready to let someone else have the room, or are you going to need some privacy for the night?"

"Nah, that would make my fiancée jealous, and she's had enough to worry about with me being shot at and chasing killers. I'm good." Ryan backed up and his anger deflated, while his face changed to a blank, emotionless mask as he walked us out.

"Crap, is that the correct time? I've got a date I'm supposed to meet at seven." There was less than an hour to get across town in traffic without causing a wreck on the way.

"Call him. Tell him you got stuck and will be a little late." Ryan went back toward the office we'd been in before.

"Well, it's our first date, but now I need to spend the evening going over everything I can find about zodiac symbols and meanings. Plus, I'm not sure I would be very good company knowing that someone else is out there that needs our help."

"No matter how hard we work, sometimes we just can't save everyone," Joe tried to reassure me as Ryan walked back toward us.

"Here. These are the numbers that will reach me or anyone on the task force without having to go through the front desk. Let's do a conference call at about nine in the morning to exchange information." Ryan handed us both a reference list of numbers for the department as a peace offering.

"You had her followed, didn't you?" I accused.

His eyes widened slightly, but he didn't take the bait. "Wouldn't you like to know?" Then he ignored me completely. "Does that work for you, Detective Roland?"

"I think we can see where we stand, and if we're any closer to a suspect. Thanks for letting us sit in on that. It was...enlightening." Joe walked toward the front.

"Don't worry. It's obvious what you're thinking, that she's just a crazy lady and doesn't have any bearing on this case. I'm going to prove you wrong," I warned as I turned on my heel and left. Without a backward glance behind me to see if he was watching, I kept walking. I wouldn't give him the satisfaction.

· · · ● ● · ● ● · ·

Once the car doors had shut and I started the engine, I was suddenly determined to make it to my date. I wasn't going to let Ryan keep me from a potentially good evening or a better mood.

"So, there seemed to be some tension between the two of you at the end of the interview," Joe accused, his tone dripping with sarcasm.

"It's a shame he can't get out of his own way and explore that there might be other possibilities out there which could help us."

"Huh. So, did the two of you become a team when I wasn't looking?"

I sighed as I maneuvered out into the last bits of downtown traffic. "I'm a horrible new partner. You're not grading me and reporting to the chief, are you?"

"No way. You're more fun than my last few partners have been. Whether you two can play nice or not, I can say for certain that the psychic cosmos lady hit one thing squarely on the head. You have chemistry and work well together. If it catches this killer, then I'm just going to sit back and watch the fireworks go off. This should be a lot of fun."

"Nope. I'm sorry to be the bearer of bad news, but there won't be any sparks between us because he has a fiancée. I'm not the kind of girl to break up a relationship, and I just might be meeting Mr. Right tonight for dinner. He's certainly going to get more of a chance than he was a few hours ago."

I wasn't going to let Ryan get under my skin. After all, I'd just met him, and there was no reason that I should care what he thought, even if the psychic had given us a reading. She hadn't said that he was the one, but we could be partners and stay alive. At least, that was the way I planned to interpret her words.

Joe was still grinning like he'd seen the best comedy act ever when I dumped him in the parking garage and raced out of there, determined to be on time for my date.

Chapter 5

Jerome was sitting at the bar when I came in, but he didn't see me. I pointed to him as the waitress got my name for a reservation.

I tapped him on the shoulder, hoping that I didn't look as rushed as I felt.

"Hey." He gave me a quick hug. "Did you put your name in with the hostess?"

"No, I wasn't sure we still had a table since I was running late."

"You're good, actually. It was a thirty-minute wait, and now we should be close to having our own booth." He waved off any apologies.

"What can I get you to drink, ma'am?" the bartender asked as I took a seat next to Jerome.

"A Dr. Pepper, no ice."

"Are you sure you don't want something to help you relax after your day?" Jerome offered nicely, pointing to his beer.

"Thanks, but I don't do much drinking because of the job. I drove over, so I'll have to have my car with me at some point," I responded as the bartender placed my soda in front of me.

"I'm sorry. I hope I didn't offend you. Being on a date with a cop is something a little different for me. Normally, you could make jokes about a lot of stuff, but I don't want you to feel uncomfortable or think I do illegal stuff."

A waitress approached. "Excuse me, sir, your table is ready. If you'll follow me."

We both picked up our drinks and followed her to a booth that gave us a little privacy.

"I'll be back in a few minutes to take your order." The waitress disappeared quickly.

"So, I'll get this out there. Just because I'm a detective doesn't mean that I'm not a person. We joke about all kinds of stuff as well. It's when it's something you do regularly that it becomes a problem. Laws are meant to be there as a guideline for those who can't make good decisions. Most people just accept the laws because it doesn't dawn on them not to, while others take joy in finding ways around them, or are just too stupid to realize that they've done something wrong." I gave him a comforting smile. "Don't be stupid, and we should get along fine."

"Ha! Well, now that we've got that out of the way, I can relax," he joked. "So, tell me about your day. From your text, I guess that things didn't go as planned?"

I chuckled. "You could say that. We had to drive to Ft. Worth because there might be a connection between some of their cases and ours. We got to interview a psychic, or gypsy. I'm not sure what she would call herself. Do you believe in that kind of stuff?"

He paused to think about it for a minute as he looked at the menu. "I guess to an extent, I do. I mean, if you follow the premise that there's a good side and an evil side, then it tends to reason that something from the afterlife would seep through to this one."

"This lady isn't so much about talking or communicating with the dead, but having visions about the future. A fore-telling, I believe they call it. I'm not sure how it all connects, but I got the feeling that she honestly believes in what she was telling us. Very down to earth, so it makes it harder to think it isn't real."

"How is she helping? By telling you who's going to be robbed or shot next?" He took a sip of his beer.

"It's an ongoing case, so I can't talk about it directly, but so far, we haven't had much luck in finding a suspect or a reason for the crimes in this case." I worded what I said very carefully, so that there weren't any details. If we had been dating or living together, I might have been able to tell him more, but I didn't trust him yet.

"On a lighter note, their pasta sampler is amazing," he suggested, steering the conversation to our date, which was thoughtful.

"I'm a fan of their Shrimp Alfredo. If you had to choose one type of food to eat for the rest of your life, what would it be?"

"Oh, I'd definitely have to go with Tex-Mex—the authentic kind, for sure. You?"

"Sweets. I'd eat anything sweet. I have a confession: when I eat by myself, I order dessert first, and then, if I'm still hungry, the entrée."

The waitress silently appeared at the table. "Here are your breadsticks. Have you had enough time to look over the menu?"

"Yes, thank you." We gave her our orders, and she walked away.

"I feel a little bit at a loss as to what to talk about next. I should have googled some first date questions," he chuckled.

"No worries. Just tell me what you like to do for fun on your days off," I prompted.

"That's easy. I like to visit new places. Since I research my day job, I like to travel. I can go anywhere, and still spend a few hours doing research, then go out and experience something different."

"Wow! That sounds like lots of fun. We did some traveling when we were younger. Now, I'm just too exhausted by the time I get off to want to go anywhere. It's not as much fun if you're doing it by yourself, anyway. I prefer to share it with someone."

Well, that didn't sound like a come-on or anything, I mentally berated myself.

"My guilty pleasure is running. It helps me stay in shape and gives me a way to run off some of my frustration when the job gets too intense."

The waitress brought our salads. "Let me see if I can get this straight. You're tied to your job, or is it that your job is tied to you?"

"I'm sorry. It's just been a while since I've been out on a date where I haven't known the person beforehand. When you become a cop, it seeps into your soul. This is an all-or-nothing kind of thing for me. Not only do I want to make the world a better place, but with all the training you do to get ready, it stays with you. This isn't the kind of job that you can leave at the door when you go home. It's not any different from being a soldier or being a mother. Once you start on that path or journey, it's something that stays with you. You can't give the baby back, and most moms that I've come across tend to keep that instinct even when the babies get older." I gave him a small smile, because if he couldn't understand that, then it would be a short date.

"No, don't apologize for being who you are. It's refreshing to have someone be upfront and honest. Speaking of that, do you have any children I should be worried about showing up at a future time?" He reached across the table to take my hand and stroke it.

"No, I don't. Not yet. I kind of knew that it was something I might want to do at a later date. How about you?" I threw the ball back into his court.

Most people our age had been in some kind of serious relationship before, and it was best to know what you were looking at if you were going to get serious.

"No children that I know of, at least. I had a girlfriend in high school that I thought was going to be the one, but things went a little differently than I'd planned. She was killed in a car crash, and I just haven't had anyone that fit right since then." He shrugged in acceptance of life's problems.

"I'm sorry." My hand gripped his hand in sympathy. "I've never lost anyone close to me before, and it would be difficult to get over, I'm sure."

We sat in silence, holding hands. I kind of liked that about this guy. He didn't seem to have a ton of expectations floating around.

"What's the strangest thing you've ever seen at a crime scene?"

"One time, we were called to a scene because of a disturbance. This guy was running down the street chasing a dog in his underwear. The dog had gone in while they were doing it and taken his pants outside through the doggy door. When he went outside to catch the dog, he ducked under the fence through a hole and took off down the street with the guy's pants. He was only visiting the house and didn't have anything else to wear." I grinned at the memory of several officers trying to block in the dog holding a pair of pants in his teeth while growling at us.

"Your turn. Craziest research question."

"Oh, how to tame the shrew." He motioned with his hands. "True story. I had to tell the guy that there was no exact method, and that he should avoid trying to tame anyone."

As we swapped horror stories, I relaxed and let my guard down a little bit. Enough that when we walked outside, I realized he was glancing at his phone instead of heading to his vehicle.

"Didn't you drive here?" I questioned curiously. I rarely used a hired car because I'd pulled too many of them over regularly to trust their driving.

"No, I don't do a lot of driving since I don't have an office that I have to go to. I prefer not to have the extra expense since I travel a lot and have to get transportation when I'm somewhere else," he explained.

"I can't imagine not having a vehicle. I'm not sure if that's because I like to be in control of my surroundings, or just that where I grew up was more rural and we didn't have taxis or other car services. You had to have a car or truck to get around."

Boldly, I looped my arm through his, pulling him toward my car. "Unless you live somewhere crazy, I'll drive you home."

"Oh, um, I wasn't expecting that. Sure, I live about ten minutes from here."

He gave me his address, and I knew the general area it was in. "Get in," I commanded.

"You sure are bossy." He grinned. "It's a good thing," he hastened to assure me.

"Right. Does that mean you're willing to go out with me again?" I headed down the street toward his house.

He rubbed his hand over his chin in a contemplative gesture, and I wondered if he'd had a beard, but shaved it recently.

"The jury was out until you offered to drive me home. Now, I'm going to say yes. Any date that is willing to make sure you get home safely is worth a second one. This is me up here on the left with the light on the side of the garage." He pointed to a quaint little house that had a cottage feel to it. "I guess this is where I leave your wonderful company."

I have no idea what came over me, but I leaned over to kiss him, and he met me halfway there.

He brought his hand up behind my head, pulling me closer as we deepened the kiss.

Whoa! That was amazing! Talk about sparks. I'd bet that Ryan couldn't kiss like that. His name running across my brain might have been the reason that I allowed Jerome to hit first base without stopping him.

I moaned as the car's center console got in my way. I pulled back, putting a hand between us. "I don't want this to be a one-night stand, so let's press pause and get a few more dates under our belts first."

"Doesn't breakfast this morning count as the first date and dinner as the second?" His fingers trailed up my arm, causing me to shiver.

Before I could answer, my phone went off, and it was my emergency ringtone.

"I guess I'll have to take a rain check. If you're free tomorrow night, we could go to my favorite Mexican food restaurant. Just text me and I'll send you the address."

He leaned in and brushed my lips with his. "Laters."

I answered the phone as he got out. "Boxe...wait, what happened? I'll be right there."

This would be a good way to see how Jerome handled being interrupted, but he hadn't seemed to mind. Maybe this dating app thing had some merit to it.

Ten minutes later, I arrived at the hospital and stopped at the desk for directions. I had to produce my badge and sign in before they would give me any information, but I made it into the emergency room only minutes before Joe arrived.

"What have we got?" he huffed, out of breath from the long walk from the parking lot and through the winding hallways.

"They've got the victim in surgery, but the husband who found her is in the E.R. waiting room. I haven't introduced myself yet."

"Ah, do we have a name?"

"Yeah." I opened the notepad on my phone. "Sarah Black. The husband's name is Ron."

Approaching the waiting room, I glanced around it, wondering how hard it would be to find the husband, but it was obvious Ron was the man pacing the room, wringing his hands anxiously.

"Ron Black?" I asked as we maneuvered past several people that were waiting to see a doctor.

"Yes." He stopped pacing. "How is Sarah? Is she going to be okay?"

"We don't know. The nurse said she was in surgery. Can you tell us what happened?" I guided him toward a few empty chairs in the corner.

"She got off early for her birthday and said that she was going to pamper herself, but that she'd be ready to go out for dinner when I got home." He sank into one of the chairs and put his head between his hands. "I stopped at a florist to get her flowers, and when I drove up, a guy was walking away from the front of the house. So instead of going in the back door like I normally would, I went to the front door.

It was open slightly, and Sarah's foot was blocking it from closing."

Wiping a tear away, he continued. "I looked at the flowers in my hand, and there beside her was another set of orchids. Disbelief was my first thought when I saw them was that she must have had a lover there, and he left. I mean, she was lying on the floor, and that's when I noticed she was bleeding. Her head was bashed in and I called 9-1-1. They said she was alive for the moment, but would need surgery." He sobbed.

We waited for him to compose himself again, but it wasn't until I pushed a box of tissues at him that he seemed to realize that we were still there.

"Mr. Black, I know this is a delicate situation. Do you think that it was your wife's lover that did this to her? Could he have been a delivery man?"

"Honestly, I would never have thought she could do this kind of thing." He sniffled and blew his nose into the Kleenex. "Even if he was the delivery guy, who else would be sending her flowers?"

"Her family isn't the type to do something like send flowers to her on her birthday?" Joe pushed him a little further.

"No, they don't have money to spend on things like that, and I don't think they even know what kind of flowers she likes." He looked confused. "This just makes no sense."

"We'll do our best to find out what happened. We're going to go over to your house and look around to see if we can find anything that might shed some light on the situation." Joe patted his knee and got up.

"Sure, whatever helps. I don't even know if I locked the door. I just got in my car and followed the ambulance here." He looked down at his clothes that were covered in his wife's blood.

"Since we have to come back here, is there anything that you'd like me to pick up for you? We'll make sure that your home is secure when we leave," Joe offered.

"Maybe another set of clothes. That's very kind of you."

"Not at all," Joe assured him, not mentioning that we'd need those clothes for evidence.

"Is there family that you need to call?" I asked as an afterthought before we left him sitting there, awaiting the outcome of her surgery by himself.

"No. Once I know something, I'll call them. I couldn't handle having her family here asking questions that I have no idea how to answer." He looked like he might break down again, so I left him sitting there forlornly.

"He doesn't seem like someone who would hurt his wife. Are we thinking this is connected to our other cases?" I followed Joe and didn't even protest about riding in his car.

"Yep. I'll bring him some clothes and we'll take those into evidence, but I don't think he had anything to do with it. He just happened to be there in time to save her life. When he's calmed down a bit, we might be able to get a description of the person he saw leaving his house."

"If we find a card with the flowers, it'll bring the attacks to eight people." I suddenly felt weary that we were fighting an uphill battle.

"Yeah, but this one is still alive," Joe injected positively.

"For the moment," I retorted without optimism.

• • ● ● ● • ● ● • • ·

Over an hour later, with nothing to show that Sarah was having an affair or company in her home to cause the attack, we arrived back at the hospital with the clean clothes for Ron, and Joe followed after him to put them straight into evidence. They had barely come out of the restroom when the doctor returned.

Ron looked up at him hopefully, but the doctor shook his head. "I'm sorry, sir, there was nothing we could do. She's gone."

"Thank you for telling me," he commented calmly before bursting into tears.

"Is there a room we could use for a few minutes?" I asked the doctor, suddenly weary.

"This way." He led us to a small room with only a few chairs.

The door hadn't even closed behind us when the doctor started explaining. "Look, when we started the surgery, it was a small chance that we were going to be able to repair the damage to her head. If she hadn't come in when she did, there's no way she'd have lived much longer. The blow to her head basically damaged her skull, and even if we had retrieved the fragments, she would have been brain dead."

Ron's sobbing lessened. "So you're telling me that I've just sat here for over two hours and let you play around in her brain when you knew there wasn't anything that you could have done to save her when you started?"

Thoroughly pissed off now, his tear-streaked face a testament to the horror he'd been through, Ron poked a finger in the doctor's chest. "Why did you give me hope that she might make it? Why not just say, 'I don't think there's much we can do before you took her into surgery?'"

The doctor edged toward the door, away from Ron's wrath. "I'm truly sorry, and I hope they can catch the one who did this to her and you." With that statement, he slipped out of the room.

"Ron, we looked around the entire inside of your home. It showed no signs of someone having had sex in the last few hours. She had taken a shower because the towel was damp in the bathroom, and all of the normal things were out on the counter after she got ready for her night out with you." I knew it wouldn't bring her back, but I wanted to ease his pain just a little bit. "Is there someone you can call?"

"I'll take a cab over to her parents and tell them in person. I'm sure they'll let me stay there since I don't think I'll be able to sleep in our home ever again." Rob swiped at his face in a futile attempt to remove the fact that he had been crying.

"We'll check in with you in the morning to see how things are going, and if you or the neighbors remember anything once you've had some rest."

It seemed so horrible to leave him alone after something like this, but we had to go to the station and fill out our reports before we forgot something important.

Nothing was standing out in a way that gave us a clue who or what these senseless killings were accomplishing.

"Joe, do you get the feeling that this guy was interrupted? Like he didn't expect the husband home quite so soon?" I sat across from him at the desk, drinking another cup of coffee to keep my brain awake.

"Yeah. He didn't plan for the husband to find her alive, that's for sure. Although, the way he's killing them isn't leaving much chance for survival. I don't want to see you back here before 9 a.m.," he admonished me.

"Yes, sir. You don't have to tell me twice." I gathered my coat and bag, ready to find my way home and to my bed.

Joe cleared the files off the desk and into a drawer before he joined me, but Nick stopped us on the way out. "Hey, the boss wants to see both of you in the morning bright and early to find out what's been going on with these murders."

"Thanks for telling us now," I groaned. "So much for an extra hour of sleep."

"If these keep going on like this, we'll be walking zombies, and maybe we'll just stumble into the killer." Joe commiserated with me as we reached our vehicles.

"See you in a few. I'll be the person walking around with a caffeine IV to keep me going."

I made the trip home on autopilot, somewhat glad that I had turned Jerome down and didn't have anyone with expectations waiting for me.

Chapter 6

The alarm sounded way too early and loud, but after years on patrol, I was able to roll out of bed and into the shower.

I hadn't even walked into the station when my phone rang, signaling another murder.

When I got to the scene, I was pleasantly surprised to find that it wasn't connected to our other cases. Two people had been arguing, and it had escalated into one of them being dead while the other was wounded.

It was a simple matter of taking statements, pictures of the crime scene, and arresting the spouse who'd been taken to the hospital. We'd placed her under arrest and would let her lawyer decide if it was self-defense since her husband wasn't there to give his side of the story. From the doctor's reports about her medical files, this wasn't the first time she'd been to the hospital with injuries, but that wasn't for us to decide.

Having been up late, it was a relief to have something that didn't need a lot of brainpower to deal with and a suspect in custody. Come to think of it, this was the first arrest that we'd made since I'd gotten my new badge. On a normal patrol shift, I might make a few arrests in one day, or only a few for the entire week.

"You know we still have to meet with the boss after lunch, right?" Joe dropped into his desk chair with a thud. "The more we have to do these late nights and early mornings, the more I dream about the days until retirement. Just until the end of the year, which seems like forever at the moment."

"I'm with you about getting some more sleep, but the fact that we haven't had a murder today from the birthday killer makes me worried." I drank the last drop of what was another cup of coffee in an endless amount today.

"What you should be worried about is the first briefing with the boss, and the fact that we have no leads on it yet."

"Hopefully, he'll give us some help on it so we can start some interviews with those who aren't as close to the victims. I still think that Noah Preston has something to do with Susan's death. He might even have a hand in the others as well."

"He's not known for his generosity. Although, last night's murder being added to the pile may tip the scales in our favor."

His phone rang. "Yeah? We'll be right there."

"Evidently, lunch is over. There's been a murder in Ft. Worth, and the boss wants to see us now." Joe wrapped his partially eaten sandwich up so that he could finish it later.

I hadn't been to the boss's office since the first day, which had been to accept a handshake and 'welcome to homicide' before being shown to my desk. This visit had a slightly different feel to it.

"Joe, why are there more bodies dropping out there? Can't you handle this without bringing in Ft. Worth? If this keeps up for even a day or two more, we're going to have the FBI showing up and sticking their noses into our business. What are you doing to make sure that doesn't happen?" The boss ripped into Joe with the door open so everyone could hear what was happening.

"My new partner found some very similar characteristics that matched those in Ft. Worth, and we went over to see if we were chasing the same killer. It appears he struck there first and they have no leads, but he chose to move around and now we have him here."

"Here? In cuffs? Then you don't have him here." Boss almost came out of his chair in frustration.

"We have a few leads that we're working on, but there's no evidence left behind, and we can't find a motive. The only thing these murders have in common is that they're killed on their birthdays by being bludgeoned to death."

It impressed me that Joe wasn't backing away from his anger, but continued to act like this was normal, and maybe it was.

"We could use a few more heads to see if they have any other ideas and help with the second set of interviews. Someone somewhere saw something," Joe concluded.

"Well, you're going to get what you asked for. Ft. Worth has requested that we send someone over there to work with them. So, Boxe, you're going to split your time between the two stations. Nick and two others are going to be assigned to you because this killer has to be taken down before the news gets ahold of the story. We don't want women who were born during this month to be living in fear." He looked between the two appraisingly.

"I'll want a daily report on my desk about what's going on with our investigation and with theirs." He pointed contemptuously in the direction of Ft. Worth.

"Yes, sir," we both responded.

"That will be all. You're dismissed." He motioned us out.

I waited until we were out of hearing range. "Is he always so pleasant?"

"He's not known for being nice, but he knows how to get the job done. He's not a fan of the homicide division's chief because they dated the same woman at the same time. She dumped the boss and stayed with the one over there. It's like a rivalry between the two cities' homicide divisions. They both want to be the one to have their name showing the best ratings," Joe explained, unwrapping his now cold burger and taking a bite.

"Guess I'll leave now and spend the afternoon over there, seeing if Ryan has anything that I can help with." I gathered the files that I had out, not looking forward to this inner-city cooperation.

Most of my afternoon was spent getting permission and filling out forms that would allow me access to the Ft. Worth building. Then, finding my way around to where each of the murders had taken place. I parked in front of the third one when my phone rang.

"Hey, how's it going today?" A smile unconsciously broke out on my face.

"Good. I was just wondering if you might like to do something tonight?" Jerome's deep voice sounded loud in my car.

"I wish I could, but I was up until almost three last night, and then had to be back in early this morning. I'm exhausted, and I don't want to rush into things like we were doing last night. I'm not trying to blow you off, I promise."

"Ah, I was wondering how late that call kept you out. What if we went to a movie so you could relax and not think about this case? No pressure. Afterward, you can go straight home and sleep."

"That might actually work."

A hired car pulled up across the street, distracting me from our conversation.

"Jerome, I'm going to have to let you go. I'll text you if we wrap things up before seven and we'll make plans. Bye."

I hung up quickly because Noah Preston was getting out of the vehicle and walking a young lady up to her door. Now, why would he be over here when he worked in Dallas at three in the afternoon? Snapping a few photos with my phone, I sent both Ryan and Joe the pictures when I realized that this was something I didn't want them to know about.

Instead, I dialed the number that Nick had given me. "Hi. I know we've never met, but I was given your phone number." I paused while he spoke. "Can you meet in about an hour at the coffee shop? Thank you."

Watching Noah get back into the car, I decided I was going to call it a day and follow him to his destination. He seemed to be the missing piece to my puzzle, and the only link I'd found so far.

• • ● ● ● • ● ● • • •

Unsure if his driver had spotted me, or if Noah had already planned to return to work, I was disappointed to find myself outside of his company's massive building back in Dallas.

A glance at my watch showed I still had almost twenty minutes to meet Ford at the coffee shop, and I wanted to give Noah a chance to get inside before I left.

He went straight to the elevator, where he met by his assistant before the doors closed and I lost sight of him.

Still trying to decide, the driver got out of his vehicle for a smoke. Jumping out of the car and acting lost, I walked toward the elevators and consulted my phone. Then, shaking my head, I walked back in the other direction and leaned over the side of the garage.

"Excuse me, sir, could you help me?" I headed closer to him. "I'm trying to find the energy department for a meeting, and I think my GPS has taken me to the wrong place."

I placed my phone where he could see what I'd typed in only a moment before.

"I'm not sure if it's the same energy place you're looking for, but there's an energy company in the main building. It's not a department, though."

"Oh, thank you. I don't want to be late for my appointment." I patted his shoulder. "You have a string on your hat. Here, let me get that for you." I stood on my tiptoes and slipped a small dot under the band of his hat. "All set."

Waiting on the elevator, I waved and turned the tracker on as the doors closed.

It was showing up loud and clear. If he was Noah's driver, then I'd have a good idea where he drove to after work. Making use of the blind spot from the parking garage, I had a car ordered and at the curb, ready to take me to my meeting with Ford.

This way, I'd be able to come back afterward and see if Noah was still in the building.

The coffee shop was mostly deserted at this time of day, except for a student or two working on papers, since it was close to one of the campuses downtown.

Knowing that more coffee was the last thing I needed right now, I ordered tea and sat down to wait for my contact to arrive.

Ford walked in, and there was no doubt that he was my contact because of his confident demeanor.

"Well, you're as gorgeous as Nick said you would be," he complimented.

"Nick hasn't been around enough women. He doesn't have a very high standard." I let the sarcasm roll off my tongue. The only way to deal with someone that had the kind of presence Ford displayed was to put up a wall to keep his charm from slipping past.

"You have the correct idea. Oh, it would be so much fun to see you let loose at our club. But I'm afraid that you would never make it long undercover. It would have to be of your own free will, and there are too many variables for that kind of project right now." Ford ran a finger up and down my arm, sending shivers over my body.

"What can you tell me about Noah Preston?" Unsure of how this worked with Nick, I decided that a forward or honest approach was the best way to work with most people.

"Straight to the point. No room for gray. Everything must be black or white." He gave a quick frown before he slipped the charm back into place.

"I'm sorry. I don't have any patience left. We have women who have been murdered, and I'm pretty sure that Noah is involved, but I just can't put my finger on any real evidence. I know it's a big ask to tell stuff about a mutual friend, but I've got to find a way to stop this killer before he takes another life," I pleaded.

"Smart and passionate as well. Hmm, I can't fault you for being suspicious of Noah. He's, what shall we say...a player? But not the good kind. He's a user, mostly. Someone who has just enough power to be dangerous, but who doesn't know how to use what he has available to him. We have very strict rules at the club. Noah has friends that overlook when he strays over the line or is too close to the rules for the rest of us. We can't do anything unless we see him do something at the club. I believe that he is keeping his more distasteful activities off-sight and avoids trouble from the board."

"He just doesn't sit well with me. He's too suave. Now, you are very charming and make women want to do whatever you demand, but he has more of a fake charm that can change when no one's looking." It clicked what I'd been feeling when I'd seen Noah.

"Astute of you to notice that. I'll ask around and see what those who've worked at one of his private parties have to say, and if there's a way for you to get what you need." He stood. "I will warn you, though. You seem to have common sense. Noah Preston is a snake and can strike with no warning. He has very powerful friends, and if they find out that you're interested in him, they can make life miserable for a new detective. Tread carefully."

With that cryptic warning, he was gone before I could process everything he'd said. My gut feeling seemed to be right on target. Noah Preston wasn't a good guy, but was he the one behind the murders?

He certainly deserved another look, but that would have to wait until tomorrow, after I went to the movies and got some sleep.

Chapter 7

J erome was waiting outside the theater, ready for a relaxing evening. I hoped I wasn't making a mistake by letting my guard down.

"You made it. What kind of movie do you want to watch?" He gave me a quick hug.

"Something light and funny, no death or guns involved." I sighed wearily.

"There's a comedy starting in ten minutes," he suggested.

"Done." I handed the ticket seller behind the glass my card.

I scooped up the tickets and headed straight to the ticket taker, but he put a hand on my arm. "Don't you want something to snack on?"

A few minutes later, we were settling into our seats with drinks and popcorn.

"This is so weird. I'm not used to going to the movies with a guy." I placed my drink opposite Jerome and turned back to find the armrest gone.

"I thought you could be more comfortable without it there."

"So, is this your way of sliding an arm behind me when you stretch?" I grinned at his none too subtle attempt for us to get closer.

"It's not like we have a lot of people watching what we're doing."

"All right." I surprised myself by leaning my head on his shoulder and putting my feet up on the seat in front of me.

Three previews later, and I remember shaking my head, knowing I'd dozed off for a second.

"What did I miss?" I sat up, trying to wake up.

"Only the entire movie." He grinned as the lights came on.

"You're serious?" I slapped at his arm. "Why didn't you wake me up?"

"Really? I knew you were exhausted and needed the sleep. Plus, it's been a while since I've had a girl curled up in my arms. It was nice," he answered sheepishly.

Stretching, I got most of the kinks off my shoulders and neck. "Now that I'm awake, do you want to get dinner?"

"If you don't think it's too forward, I'd like to pick up something and go back to my house. You mentioned you needed to do some research, and that's what I do for a living. So maybe we can eat while you get some insight into your case," Jerome offered generously.

"Wow! That would be amazing. I also promise I won't fall asleep on you after dinner."

"Great, it's decided then. I know just the place and can call an order in while you drive over to pick it up."

"This dating thing might not be as bad as I'd thought when I signed up for it."

Dinner was over, and instead of trying to seduce me, Jerome brought a laptop over and sat it on the coffee table in front of us.

"Some things I have folders on because the magazines or papers do a lot of stuff based on certain subjects. What are you wanting more information on?" His fingers hovered over the keys, ready to type in whatever I said.

"Okay, I'm going to give you a subject that keeps coming up, but you can't speak about it to anyone," I warned. This would be a good test to see if he could keep things to himself. A good relationship between us wasn't going to work if he wasn't trustworthy enough to ignore things he might pick up on from my job.

"No worries. You're so far off the record that I won't even remember what I looked up for you." He mimed zipping his lips and throwing the key away.

"I need to know more about the birth sign, Aquarius." I took a deep breath, hoping I wasn't about to lose my job.

"Okay. Well, I do know a little bit about it. Most papers run a horoscope reading daily or weekly, depending on your sign. You can also access that online and get a daily reading from one of the top psychics in the states." He pulled up a few sites for me to look at.

"These look like generic things that might happen to anyone in a day. It's just a gimmick for someone to come back daily or pay more money to have a personalized reading," I muttered suspiciously.

"Each city has a sign based on its latitude and longitude, when it was established, among other things."

"See if you can find what sign Dallas has, or Ft. Worth," I urged, interested in the results.

"It says here that Dallas and Ft. Worth are Sun Aquarius signs. Does that mean something to you?"

"Yes," I answered shortly. "Each of the murders that we've uncovered has been done when the sun was still up. I hadn't even thought about it. The bodies might not have been discovered until after dark, but each attack was during daylight hours. What else does it say?"

"Hmm, there are lots of details about love and which partners are the best matches. Each sign even has a preferred flower and color."

"What flower is the one for Aquarius?" I had a sinking feeling that it would be orchids.

"Orchids are the sign's flower."

"Shit!" I didn't cuss that much, but there were times when it was needed.

"It says that they hate injustice and work well with innovation, philanthropy, conserving energy, and making the world a better place."

There was that word 'energy' again, and it was coming up more than once. But I turned my focus back to what Jerome was describing.

"They tend to be very independent while not wanting to be alone. They may settle for the wrong person simply so they're not by themselves. Most work well with others in a team situation, but don't like having an overbearing boss that will cause them to rebel." Jerome had no idea how many things she could use to find reasons why these women had been murdered.

"There's more technical stuff that has to do with the rotation of the sun and the alignment of the stars, but most of that is over my head. It would take a few hours before I could gather enough information for it to make sense to someone without that kind of background. Psychics are often firm believers in people's signs and what it means for their futures."

"Unbelievable. I'm going to have to go back to the psychic and see what kind of information she may have that could help me get into this killer's mind." I had a way to get Flora's contact info, but I was pretty sure that it was going to mean having a conversation with Ryan to get to the bottom of her story.

"Sorry, I didn't mean to overwhelm you with so many details. This is so fascinating." Jerome could barely pull himself away from the computer screen.

"Why don't you keep doing some research, and I'll go home and get some rest? I think my nap worked for a small while, but I'm starting to fade again." I got up and grabbed my bag from the side of the couch.

My words brought his attention back to the present. "Don't go."

"I have to. Even though you're amazing, I need some rest because I don't think this killer is going to stop anytime soon. Thank you for a lovely evening. I'm sorry I fell asleep during the movie," I apologized, walking to the front door.

He joined me, but put a hand on my arm to stop me from leaving. Instead, he gave me a kiss that had my toes tingling from the heat of it.

"You don't play fair," I groaned, reaching for the door handle to escape what could become a welcome moment in his bed.

"Nope, no pressure. That was just so you wouldn't forget about me while you sleep." He gave me a cocky grin.

"Have no fear. I couldn't forget something that steamy even if I wanted to."

Tearing myself away, I raced to my car and slid behind the wheel, feeling like I'd escaped something.

Yeah, a night of amazing sexual pleasure.

That brought me back to the present because my phone beeped with an update on where Noah was at the moment. So much for a night of sleep.

Chapter 8

I arrived early enough to type up my report for the boss with some information about similarities between the murders, and that they had all been done during daylight hours.

Joe wasn't in yet, but I still had the drive over to the other station to meet Ryan.

While I was driving to Ft. Worth, trying to avoid the traffic going to work, I replayed the trail Noah had left behind. I'd managed to intercept him and follow behind at a discreet distance. He'd gone to the club while I'd been at Jerome's, but when I found his vehicle ahead of me, he'd pulled into a housing section where two of the murders had happened.

He'd walked a woman up to her door before going back to the car and pulling away. Since I'd seen that she was alive when I left, I had to wonder how long he toyed with them before he had them murdered. I was pretty certain that he wasn't the one actually doing the killings. It would be more

likely that he'd have them disposed of by someone he trusted.

Someone cut in front of me, reminding me that I needed
to have something grounded in reality.

When I'd walked into the other station and gone through
all the security checks, it was like I'd started all over again.

Ryan's office wasn't difficult to find since I'd been there
before, but he was walking out as I was about to knock on
the door.

"We just caught one, and the neighbors are the ones who
called it in. You can ride with me." His commanding tone
made me bristle inside.

"Sure," I managed to respond politely.

Unlike most of the other murders, this one was on the bad
side of town at an apartment.

"When things happen in this neighborhood, we normally
have a hard time finding anyone who saw what happened.
Evidently, this wasn't typical because we had five phone calls
about it. The victim was dead when we got there, but we
might have a description since they're not feeling threatened
to keep quiet about it," Ryan explained as he expertly maneuvered into an empty parking spot.

"Not gang or drug-related, and she must have been someone they all cared about or they wouldn't have bothered."

"Bingo! That is what we've been waiting for was someone
to lay eyes on this killer." He got out, taking charge of the
patrol officers on the scene.

A small crowd had gathered on the lower level of the apartment complex and was hovering on the sidewalk. I edged closer to listen to what they were saying.

"We've never had someone hurt one of our own like that," an older man grumbled.

"Bert, you know that's not true. She was a hussy and had men coming to see her all the time. This is the kind of thing that happens when you answer the door, no matter if you know them or not."

"Gina, you're just jealous that she was getting some, and us old coots know better than to mess with you. If we wanted to be nagged to death, we'd have stayed married to our first wives." Bert chuckled and nudged his buddy standing next to him.

"How did she get hurt?" I asked curiously.

Half of those standing there gave me a dirty look. A white girl in business attire wasn't something they normally saw taking part in conversations like this.

"Why do you want to know?" Gina asked, her tone suspicious.

"I got the report on the radio and beat the news cameras over here. Can you give me the scoop?"

"Hmph. In my day, a lady wouldn't be seen in public without dress shoes on, but I guess you can't expect everyone to be professional these days." She raised an eyebrow as she looked me up and down.

I didn't want to tell her that the purple she'd used as brow liner to fill in the thinning areas wasn't how it was done, but I thought I'd ignore it if it got us some answers.

"Never mind, Gina, she's just a grouch. We were all in our apartments when we heard a loud scream, or at least I did. Normally, you don't pay much attention so they don't look your way, but this was so early in the morning, and most of the problems are in the late afternoons and evenings. Anyway, I peeked out my window and saw this guy running past." Bert paused, and his friends took up the story.

"Once the guy was gone, we knew it was safe to see what was wrong, and only three people live on the end down there. We have a pretty good idea who belongs to which place, but I never expected to see Joy lying there with blood just pouring from her head."

"Everyone was afraid to move her, but I could tell by her eyes that she was already gone. Even though others..." Bert glanced toward Gina, "were busy calling 9-1-1."

"Did she have any enemies?" I urged them to keep going.

"No, but it was a regular revolving door of men. Sometimes it was the same one, but never for more than a week or two. She was just the sweetest thing," a man in the group added.

"Oh, I did notice the killer get in his car. It was a gray van that had 'florist' written on it," Bert gushed excitedly.

"Was he wearing anything distinctive?" I cautioned myself, as I didn't want to lead them in any specific direction.

"He didn't fit in because he didn't have a uniform on, but was wearing khakis and a polo shirt." Gina wanted to make sure to put her two cents in. "He wasn't all that good-looking, but I guess it takes on all types."

"Thank you. It might help catch her killer." I excused myself to go see if Ryan had anything at the crime scene.

"Wonder why they let her past the yellow tape?" Gina complained loudly.

"Aw, she's got to try to get a statement from the detective." Bert pointed to the balcony that wasn't dripping with blood anymore.

"Where's the camera crew?"

I only caught the question posed to their huddled group. I felt sorry for them because while it was probably more excitement than they were used to; they were lucky they hadn't tried to stop our killer or they might be on the way to the hospital.

The stairs took me out of sight for a few minutes, but the scene was already way too familiar.

Her body was lying outside the door in a pool of blood and brains.

"She fought back. That's why she's out here instead of inside. He might have startled her, but she managed to shove him outside before he could actually hit her." Ryan straightened from crouching next to the body where he'd been examining her.

"There were flowers inside. Is there a card?" I took out a pair of gloves before I stepped through her doorway.

"Haven't gotten to it yet. Where did you disappear to?"

"Her neighbors had a few things to add to the story they were telling to a reporter."

"You told them you were with a news station?" Ryan questioned angrily.

"No, I told them I beat the camera crews here and asked if they could tell me what happened."

Nodding, he looked surprised. "Not bad for a newbie."

"They wouldn't speak to the police, but a chance to be quoted for the news is a different matter." I winked at him. "I might be new to this, but I wasn't born yesterday."

"Touché."

"Ah, here's the card." I pulled it out of the shattered glass lying in the doorway among the flowers.

"Same as the others?" Ryan asked.

"Yep. I'm wondering what made her fight instead of taking the flowers? Her neighbors seemed to think that she was well acquainted with strange men showing up all the time."

"It's not uncommon in this area, but I'll check with vice and see if they have any idea who might have been frequenting her apartment lately." He added a note to his phone.

"That's something that's always bothered me."

"What bothers you?" he questioned as he followed me down the stairs.

"How many man-hours does vice spends to watch a flop-house or drug house when they could just arrest those that are in it and be done with it? They could move on to another area of crime." His face was the perfect picture of shock. "I know, it's all so we can get the big fish, but if we arrested all the little fish, then the big fish would go out of business and take care of the problem from a different perspective."

"What on earth made you become a cop?" Ryan asked incredulously as he got in the car.

"My big sister's one," I confessed.

"Oh, the hero. Or should I say, heroine worship got to you?"

"Yeah, it's not that I don't think we're doing something good—I do. There are just better ways for that to happen that don't allow the crimes to continue at the cost of the victims."

"Sounds like you would be on board with your new police chief who's redoing the vice department over there."

Ryan didn't sound too thrilled at the rumors he'd heard.

"Have to wait and see if her new plans will work out the way she expects them to. But you don't make any progress without some trial and error."

"True, but at what cost to the system that's already in place?"

"Hey now, we both know that there are problems with the system. It's not something that can be changed overnight. Each little pebble you throw causes a ripple, so you have to choose well. That way, you have a greater impact on the right side."

He shook his head at my idealist views. "You'll lose most of that after you've been on the job for a while. It's a hard life, which is why you're about to meet my fiancée for a quick lunch."

"Oh, you're engaged. See? You're not completely hardened beyond repair," I teased.

"She's one of the few that's been able to deal with my long and erratic hours."

"Had a few that you took for a test drive first, huh?" I couldn't explain the comfortable way he made me feel, and I wasn't worried that I was going to hurt his feelings.

"Ha-ha, very funny. I meant in the police world, not personally. We've been together for about five years now. The plan is to get married sometime next year because she knows where she wants to get married, but she has to find an open date." He shrugged. "It's her wedding, and honestly, I have things like murders to solve, so I leave all the details to her."

"Is that what she wants, though? Not having you around, even just to listen, must be tough." Every girl dreamed about their weddings and how they wanted it to look, but they still liked to have the guy involved a little bit.

"Nah. She knows that some days I have more energy than others, depending on the caseload. It's what you'll have to get used to as a new detective. Having a relationship is hard in this job."

"I just met someone and we've been on a few dates. I don't know how he'll react if I cancel or reschedule regularly. He's been amazing, but I know that's just the way things work in any relationship."

"So you're dating?" He darted a glance in my direction without taking his eyes off the road for more than a second.

I cocked my head to the side and looked out the window as I contemplated the idea that I might be in a relationship. "It's too early to call it that, but we have been on a few dates now."

He pulled up in front of a sandwich shop.

"I'll just stay in the car so I don't intrude."

"No way. I already told her about you, and the fact that you simply had that psychic lady eating out of your hand. She's eager to meet you."

"I'll just bet she is," I mumbled softly.

In my experience, when a wife or girlfriend wanted to meet you, that meant they were checking out your hotness level to see if you were a threat while working with their husbands. It didn't always turn out bad or cause the changing of partners, but most of the time, my partner suddenly needed to be in a different division without any explanation.

Making friends was hard to do, but having friends that were girls was almost impossible. I was more like one of the guys than a girly girl.

"Well, I might as well get it over with and get some food out of it." Plastering a smile on my face, I went to have another friendship killed before it even got started.

Ryan approached a booth with a petite woman, who did not fit my image of a blonde model that was floating around in my head. Shea was a blonde but had that shy, introverted manner about her.

"Hey, babe." He kissed her forehead. "I'd like you to meet Leslie Boxe, the one that's been working the case with me."

She had a bite of food in her mouth, and hurriedly placed a napkin up to cover her face.

"It's so nice to meet you." She held out her left hand, which signified that she was a lefty.

"Hi. I'm sorry, he just told me we were stopping. I would have gotten something at the station so that you two could have a meal together."

"Don't worry yourself about it. Ryan is always trying to find minutes where we can squeeze some time in together. I enjoy meeting the people he works with so that I know his partner's got his back. Anything can happen, and it's important to have someone to look out for you."

"We'll go ahead and order now, but don't wait for us to eat your food." Ryan headed to the counter to place his order.

Most of the food looked good in the pictures. I mean, how badly could someone mess up a sandwich, right?

I took a seat across from the two of them and watched their body language. People watching was a hobby that most cops used, even when they weren't on duty. It was just second nature.

Ryan had his arm around her, while she had a hand on his leg.

Jealousy hit me with a quick stab of pain. Not that they were together, but that I didn't have someone like that yet. The relationship with Jerome was only in the early stages.

"What do you make of our case? Any ideas on how this person is so successful at committing these murders with almost no witnesses—until today, that is?" Ryan took a bite of his sandwich.

"I've researched the astrology sign on the cards. It appears that our psychic, Flora, might have a point. The flowers that he brings are always orchids, which are more common this time of year, and the flower of the Aquarius sign."

"Well, don't stop now. Go on," Ryan urged, as he and Shea stopped eating to listen.

"All right. There seems to be a pattern to this killer. He only kills during the daytime, and both Ft. Worth and Dallas are considered Sun Aquarius cities."

"What the hell is a sun city? How did they become sun cities? Is this why he's choosing them?" Ryan sputtered.

"Honey, if you'd let her talk, you might find some answers." Shea winked at me.

Taking a deep breath so that I didn't take his frustration personally, I began again. "From the research, we did last night—"

"We who?" Ryan demanded.

"My date, who happens to research for a living. Actually, I only told him I was looking into astrology and the signs because I'd had to interview a psychic and wanted to see if her predictions were on point. It was case adjacent, and he didn't get any of the details about the murders." I looked pointedly from him to Shea, and then around the room filled with strangers. There was no one in the booths around us, but there were a few other people in the room.

"She has a point, Honey. I'm here listening, and it sounds like she told him a lot less about it than I know."

"Well, I trust you. I know you and I just met her, and I've never met her guy. They aren't even in a relationship. How do we know he's not the killer?" Ryan protested.

Before I could protest, Shea did it for me. "Honey, I know that you don't trust people easily. I also know that your instinct is telling you to trust Leslie, and you're not doing it. She wouldn't have made it to detective or been assigned to help you if she wasn't good at her job." She shook a finger under his nose. "You also know that you've pumped for information or gotten help from many people about cases that had no idea what you were looking for, so don't be putting your issues onto her. She doesn't deserve it."

Shea turned to me. "I'm going to go, but I want you to know that underneath all his crap is a nice man. If you can make it past that, the two of you should work fine together.

It was nice meeting you, and I'm sure that I'll see you in the future—if he doesn't run you off."

I held out my hand to her. "It was a pleasure, and I have to say, you're the better half. I won't be going anywhere until these murders are solved."

Ryan just sat there after she left, picking at his sandwich.

"Were you going to eat that?" I tried not to giggle, knowing that it would piss him off more.

Men weren't all the same, but there were some characteristics that most seemed to have, and being reminded to have manners by your future wife would always cause their pride to be hurt.

"Yeah. Why don't you finish telling me what you and your 'date' found," he mumbled between bites.

That was the most of an apology I could expect for now, but he wasn't going to get off so easily next time. Besides, I had his fiancée to back me up.

"Sure. Where was I before I was interrupted...Oh, sun cities. They're formed due to the date they were created—the cities, that is. When a city is formed, they are given an astrological sign that's determined on the date and time, as well as the geographical location of the cities' center. Some cities were around for years before they became established. They don't get a sun or a moon sign until the actual declaration or contract between the city officials makes the charter."

When he didn't say anything, I continued. "It just so happens that both Ft. Worth and Dallas are sun cities for

Aquarius. This is allowing the killer to move between the two cities and makes it harder to anticipate his moves. If I hadn't done that search based on M.O.'s, we might not have made the connection, and the crimes might not have been linked."

He gave me a tight nod and took another bite of food. I'd have to remember that he shut down when he was mad or upset.

"I think that if we look at all the women in our cases, we're going to see a pattern between many aspects of their lives."

"Now hold on. How could he have watched or known about these particular women? Even if they're born under the sign of Aquarius, that doesn't mean that they don't have their own personalities. It's not like there's a directory of people who are born on this date," Ryan protested.

"Well, actually, there is. Online, you can find out just about anything about anyone. Some of it's not exactly legal, but most of it can be found out with a subscription or membership to the site. There are databases about all sorts of things, including social media, that will bring up the information that he needed to find these girls. Stalking is much easier than most people think it is, no matter how much protection or privacy you put on an account."

"So we're back to square one again. Great. So your research didn't find anything?" Ryan collected his trash and got up to throw it away.

I waited patiently for him to take his seat again before continuing. "Exactly the opposite. We know that he has to be getting flowers from somewhere every day. It's the same arrangement, so we can check to see if he's ordering them or having them sent somewhere and then picking them up. We might not be able to trace how he found his victims, but we can run a search for each city and see who checks the boxes for what he's been looking for."

Ryan frowned. "Let's discuss this in the car on the way back to the station. We can find out if your idea has merit when I put a few of the guys to calling flower shops."

"I'm going to text Joe so they can do that in our area, but we need to find a way to get a warrant for the national flower orders from online."

"Hmm...I'll talk to my boss and get the approval to order the warrant. Since it's a national company, I can't guarantee that we'll get an agreement, but if we narrow it down to only that type of flower order in our two cities and only delivered this month, that might make a difference as well."

"We might catch a break on the individual shops, and he might have ordered from the same few." I was relieved because I hated to do warrants. They were never my favorite part because they need technical details, and it wasn't something I was great at. Which might be why mine didn't get approved very often.

Once inside the car and Ryan was distracted, I mentioned something I didn't want to say where there might be other listening, and he couldn't get upset about it. "I also think most of these women were doing some type of good deeds. The psychic mentioned that this was a great evil meant to take the good away. What if each of these women were involved in something that socially affected others? Like they volunteered at the soup kitchen, or donated to those that were down on their luck. If each of these women were gone, then the good deeds they were doing would be taken away, and those that had been surviving because of their generosity would take a turn for the worse."

"You believe her, don't you?" Ryan glanced over with a frown.

"Maybe not 'believe,' but if we follow her logic, it makes sense in a twisted way."

"How on earth could our lady of the night have been a philanthropic person? What did her death do to affect others besides her own family, who might even be relieved that she wasn't going to end up in more trouble than she was in before?" Ryan's tone dripped with disbelief and cynicism.

"When I talked to those older men, they had nothing bad to say about her. I know they appreciated her looks. Being old men and all, they aren't completely blind yet. They wouldn't have been worried when they heard her scream or run to help her. You said that the neighborhood is terrible, and you were surprised that I'd gotten any information from them. Maybe it's because she meant more than your average hooker did."

He shook his head. "Again, I can't believe they sent me a dreamy cop, but you might have a point. You got more information about her with your news story cover than I could have gotten in multiple interviews. Much as I hate to do this, why don't you go back over there this afternoon and see if you can find a reason that she was well-loved, or at least liked for a hooker."

The surprise must have shown on my face because he got defensive. "I don't believe in all this hoodoo about the cosmos, but it doesn't mean that we can't take what she said and work it to our advantage."

"I'll take it, and if it means that we catch a killer, then all the better. I think we should call her back in and have a chat to see what else she might know. She mentioned that she didn't read palms, but that she advised financial people about their futures. Both can't be right, so I want to see if we can find how she's lying."

"You've been playing me, having me think you believed her. Why haven't we been questioning her?" Ryan's outrage was only for show, but he played it well.

"She's had a tail on her since we talked to her, and if something unusual had happened, you'd have already brought her in. But you can't find anything, and it's making you cranky."

"If you keep that up, I might think you're the psychic. Maybe they didn't make a mistake with your promotion."

All I could do was raise an eyebrow. Ryan was making me so tired. I had no idea why I'd been jealous earlier because, after only a short time, I pitied Shea for all the emotional rollercoasters Ryan went through in a short while.

This partnership might just keep me single for a while longer, although sex with Jerome was beckoning on the horizon, and it had been a long time.

Chapter 9

It took me a little longer to find Joy's apartment complex, but I sat there for just a minute watching the inhabitants as they interacted. The older guys sat in lawn chairs in the courtyard, commenting on all the children that weren't being watched by parents. A few doors were open, and a mom would stick her head out and tell them to quit screaming, which didn't faze them in the least.

A gate blocked my way to the entrance of the courtyard, but I had to think back to earlier. I hadn't remembered there being a gate I had to open to go upstairs.

Bert, the other guy from earlier, and two old guys were sitting around in sturdy chairs that didn't seem to fit with the rest of the rundown appearance of the complex.

They noticed me when I pulled an extra chair up to their circle and sat down.

"Well, look here, Bert. The pretty news lady came back," the guy chuckled. "Told you she was real nice." He gestured to the others sitting there. "I didn't get to introduce myself earlier. I'm Johnny. This here is George, and that old coot is Fred. You remember Bert."

"I'm Leslie Boxe." I held out my hand as I introduced myself.

"Nice to meet ya, but they were saying the news van never got here. Wasn't Joy's death enough to make the news?" Fred took my hand accusingly.

"Oh, I just said that I beat the camera vans. I'm not that kind of reporter. I don't like being in front of cameras, and yes, Joy's death deserves to make the news. I've got some questions that I couldn't ask earlier, as I had to do some research. Would you mind answering a few more?" I smiled at each one of them, hoping they would take my excuses.

Bert rubbed his beard thoughtfully. "I guess it couldn't hurt if it helps you catch this guy that killed her."

"Did Joy do anything like volunteer at a soup kitchen or other social work?" I held a small notebook on my lap to write down their responses.

The four men looked at each other and seemed to have a silent conversation between them, before Fred answered slowly, "This won't get anyone in trouble, will it?"

"What do you mean? Was she doing something illegal?"

I realized the question would make them stop talking, so I rephrased it. "Besides what she did for a living, was there something else that she was involved in that might have gotten her killed? I'm not looking to get anyone arrested. Joy's dead, and as far as I'm concerned, you're just reliable sources. See? I don't even have your names written on here." I pointed to the few notes that didn't have anything to do with this case on it.

"Okay, then." Fred nodded reluctantly. "She was our benefactress."

"Fred thinks that just because he used to be an extra in a movie they filmed years ago, that he should use all these big words and talk down to the rest of us," George spoke for the first time. "You'll have to excuse him. Joy was one of the reasons that we're out here watching the children."

Keeping a straight face, I listened as George took over the conversation.

"Joy had a system going that she thought would benefit us all and make it a little easier to stay under the gangs and cop's radars while keeping us alive."

"She approached us retired or disabled older folks, and asked if we could help some moms who worked to watch their children. The moms would pay us in groceries, and that way, they didn't have to pay for daycare. She bought some gates and had them installed so the kids could play in the yard," Johnny chimed in. "So we aren't getting paid for what we do and don't have to report it, but extra groceries are always welcome."

"Why, she even talked to a few of the younger group and got them to help with the school-agers, offering to pay them instead of having them sell drugs." Bert blushed before he continued. "I know that she had a deal for protection with one of the gangs. She'd give them a certain amount of free hours of her intimate time a week if they would stay outside the complex."

"I was under the impression that this neighborhood wasn't such a great one to live in because of the gangs..." I paused. "I don't mean anything against your home, but it's not a safe place to raise a family."

They all started nodding in agreement. "You're right. Before Joy moved in last year, this complex was horrible, but after she took over managing it, things turned around. Now, if you go over to the next complex, it's exactly what you say—unsafe."

"Hold on...she was the manager of the apartments? Why did she live up here? Most managers live off-site, especially for a complex like this."

"That's what we always asked her, but she said that if you want to change the world, you have to start small and work your way up." George turned to wipe a tear away.

"Just don't report us. We don't know what will happen now that she's gone," Johnny pleaded, his voice trembling.

Bert's darker, the wrinkled face grew grave. "The gang leaders will stay back for a while, and might even take money if we offered, but we're all broke. When that killer took our Joy, they did it both literally and figuratively."

"Now look who's using big words," George teased.

"I'm very sorry for your loss, and don't worry, I won't turn you in because you're not doing anything wrong. If Joy was trading favors, then that would be on her and not you guys. But if I think of something that will keep the gangs away from all of you, I'll let you know."

I bid them all goodbye and drove my car away, trying not to cry. I knew that if I started, I wouldn't be able to stop. Flora was right about the darkness filling the air; it was a depression that was growing rapidly.

• • • ● • ● ● • • •

Ignoring Ryan's voice in my head, I drove over to the campus housing that Flora lived in to see what else I could learn from her.

She lived in a cute duplex and was just walking up to her home as I pulled up.

"Flora!" I called out, getting her attention.

"Hi, Leslie. I'm not under arrest, am I?" She laughed as she continued toward the house. "Would you like to come in?"

She didn't know that by inviting me inside, anything I saw that was incriminating could be used against her, but that wasn't my problem.

"Thank you. I've been bothered by this killer and the fact that he's using a zodiac sign. If we could figure out why he's doing this, it would make it much easier to find him."

I followed her into a brightly decorated room that smelled of incense.

"There's not much I can tell you that I haven't already, but I don't think that's why you're here, is it?" She pointed to an empty overstuffed chair.

I sighed. "You're right. I'm conflicted. I just met someone, and he seems nice, but Ryan is someone that challenges me. He's taken, though, and I don't want to just be settling for second best. What makes it worse is that his fiancée is nice."

"I'm not hearing what the conflict is about. You have two guys to choose between, and you're not sure where your heart is leading you?" she asked, giving me an appraising stare.

"It's too early to have feelings, but don't I want someone that challenges me? Although, since I met him, Jerome has been the most patient man I've ever met. All of this is starting to weigh on me. This is why I try not to date." I groaned to myself, not expecting her to answer.

"Each brings his own brand of personality to the table, and you'll have to choose what you need the most. I'd wait to make any decisions until you've had sex. It can change the way you feel in a lot of ways. I think the way will be shown to you if you are patient. I know that it's hard to do, and to hear everyone tell you the same thing over and over, but it's the way the world works."

"Is it too selfish to want the romance and the fireworks?" I held up two hands, weighing each thought on a different hand.

"I think you should give it a week before you make any decisions. Let me help you with this other problem, and it will clear your mind of all the other things that are distracting you. Murder is against what the universe is comfortable with, and so this man will be marked in his own way. It doesn't necessarily mean that he's mental or has a physical mark, but he could."

"I'd take just one thing that could lead us toward him. We know some of the details, but there are still too many variables out there."

"Between school and research, I'm afraid that I haven't found anything that could help you so far."

"You don't have to make excuses, I understand. School comes first."

"No, you don't understand. I've been going to school, but this darkness and the visions are getting worse. I'm not sure that I can control this kind of karmic vibrations from this killer."

"What do you mean? I'm not acquainted with how that works."

"Each time someone dies a violent death, the cosmos mourn for them. Revenge and retribution cannot be handled by someone close to them. This killer has a plan and a timetable. Each of his kills has been precise and thought out. The one victim that was alive might have been able to describe his face. You're sure that it's a male, correct?"

"Yes, ma'am."

"This is a ritual to him, and that's the reason things are done in the same manner over and over again. He's got this down to an art and knows just how long he has before someone notices that the victims are dead. He's very bold."

"See, my partner mentioned that the other day. Why do you think he's bold? Aren't all hired killers?" I hadn't thought of the possibility that he might have some characteristics that we could track easily.

"He walks boldly in the sun and doesn't worry about the consequences. This is all new to me, and intertwined with what I'm studying—psychology. Before last month, I'd had strong feelings about things, but never like this. When someone would ask for advice, I could always tell what they needed to do."

"You said that you've helped businessmen. What does that mean, exactly?" I watched her curiously to see if she was as relaxed as she looked.

"When I started school, I was going for a business degree because that's a stable thing to have. I interned with a few companies, and when I was in the break room, I'd overhear something and make a comment. It might not even be big or important, but the person would use what I'd said. The next thing I knew, everyone was coming to me for advice. It was driving me crazy because some of the things I saw weren't good, but I couldn't exactly tell them that it would be a horrible decision." She shrugged, unapologetic.

"You know when you see someone, that they aren't a good person, or they're just saying they're fine, but you can tell that something is wrong? I've had that my whole life, an intuition. Some people would say it's from God, others would say it's evil. I honestly didn't know I was that different until I got to college a few years ago. We lived in a small town, and so I didn't meet a lot of new people. When I came to college, I don't think I realized that something was different until the second year. I was so overwhelmed with all the new people, ideas, and routines.

"Instead of hearing someone speak, I started to just know things about them. Nothing incredibly big or crazy, but enough to know that what I'd been feeling wasn't normal." She smiled. "I tested my feelings, or intuitions, a few times to see if they were right. Every time I was right."

"Is there some way to focus your intuitions or turn them off?" I didn't want to offend her.

"Not exactly. There are a few things I can do to keep evil from crossing my doorstep, but that's only the spirits, not actual people. I must be very naïve because I thought I was growing up, and that most people had this kind of foreknowledge. When I told a boyfriend that he needed to go home because his mother was dying, and he looked like I had grown a third head, that was when I knew I was different. I planned to ask my mother about it, but every time I brought it up over the Christmas break, she changed the subject. It made me curious, and I started studying.

"What I discovered was that those who have these kinds of intuitions, or claim to be psychic, can be related to the Romani, or gypsy, as most people call them. I've been reading up on the subject and decided to change my major since I already read people very well. I can get in their heads without anyone questioning why I would know something like that."

"That's a positive position to take. I know that the police don't look well on psychics or those who claim to be one." I was impressed.

"If that's the case, and I felt that from Detective Ryan, certainly, what makes you so different?" She sat there, patiently waiting for an answer that I'm sure she already knew.

"Honestly, it was a gut feeling for me as well. I knew you were telling the truth and genuinely wanted to help. So many times we overlook those who have the most information simply because they don't fit the profile we've put together in our brains. I can't say that I believe in listening to the universe, but there have been moments when I knew that if I went around a corner, something bad would happen. Ryan's started calling me a dreamer because I keep referring back to you."

"Oh boy. That's probably going over well, isn't it?" She laughed at the picture it painted of my co-partner.

"I don't want to offend you, but can you read people?" I blushed. "That wasn't what I meant. Like, if you saw them in a lineup, or while they were being interviewed, could you get a feeling if they were guilty?"

"It's not an exact science, and not something I've practiced yet. If the murderer was in there, then definitely. If they were just guilty of a small crime, I'm not sure how it would work. You catch him, and I'll do my best if you want me to come in."

"I'm in Ryan's district at the moment, so I'm just here on good behavior. I'll see what I can do, but I would love to have lunch at some point as you learn more about this subject. I just find it fascinating." I rose because I'd been gone longer than I'd planned, and I was supposed to go by the morgue with Ryan.

"That sounds amazing. I won't have to hide who I am from you."

"We could see who guesses the most information about someone and if they're right. Cops develop what some call a sixth sense about people, and most of it's just based on observation."

She accompanied me to the door. "If something changes, I'll let you know. For the moment, the evil I've felt is in a holding pattern, waiting for a chance to do more, but they haven't yet."

"Thank you, and I'll try to keep my personal stuff to myself so that you don't have to feel you need to offer me advice."

"Friends do that for each other no matter if they have the 'gift' or not."

"True. Stay safe, please." I turned back to call after her, but she had already shut the door.

"Now to face Ryan, but I have a pretty good idea what he'll think of this visit," I muttered under my breath.

Chapter 10

Ryan finally joined me in the break room, and his ears were steaming.

"We've been working our butts off, and the brass has the balls to think they could have solved this faster or that we've missed something. Sorry, I'm just pissed."

"Don't apologize, you're right. We have to go back over everything and see what we missed." I knew that sometimes you just had to be angry for a while, especially when there was no way to work through it.

"Start at the beginning? This means a trip to the morgue, and it might as well be now. Let's go." He took off, and for once, I meekly followed. There was always a time and place to speak up, but right now there wasn't any point in poking an angry bear.

"Did you find out anything from those old guys?" He didn't pause or slow his stride, which I appreciated.

"Sort of. She was the person doing the good deeds. She'd cleaned up the complex and was keeping the drug dealers and gangs out for a price. I called Joe while you were out and asked him to check on our side for any kind of good deeds that would make sense as a link between victims."

"At least you know enough to work without having someone hanging over your shoulder, telling you what to do next." He peeled out of the parking garage with a vengeance.

"Why don't I ask the questions this time and see if I can spot something different?" I was feeling bad for anyone that had to be in close contact with him for the next few hours, myself included.

"Sure, why not? You might find something. That's the benefit of being new. You see things that some of us would overlook because it seems too obvious."

The Ft. Worth morgue was similar to the Dallas one, but unlike those on TV, this one was aboveground and had quite a few employees working. Ryan made his way straight to the M.E.'s office.

A quick rap was all he gave before he entered, not giving anyone a chance to tell him no. "Laura, this is my temporary partner, Leslie."

"I see that, and I'm so sorry. He didn't tell you the connection. I'm Ryan's cousin, which is why he doesn't feel the need to actually knock like a civilized person. Good thing I wasn't having a nooner."

Ryan smirked. "It's three in the afternoon, and by definition, a nooner should be done around the noon hour, which is how it came by its name."

I just shook my head at his answer. "Honestly, we were hoping that you might have matched the wounds with a murder weapon. We're just groping blindly in the dark, and we haven't found today's body yet."

Laura took her seat again and waved to the chairs in front of her desk for us to sit in. "I've narrowed it down to a baton or nun chucks. They're both the right size, but most people that carry a baton use plastic, and this was definitely wood. It's not easy to hide those when doing a delivery, and I doubt he was carrying it around where the victims could see it. Other than that, there isn't any evidence that links anyone to these murders. I wish there was."

"Thank you, Laura. We'll get out of your hair and go over each one of these from the beginning again." I rose and hoped that Ryan would as well.

"Bye, Laura. Maybe we can make lunch next week if these murders slow down." He didn't wait for her reply, but stalked out of the room.

"His manners could use some work, but I know how it feels to be helpless."

"Yep. I'll keep an eye on him." I pulled the door closed behind me.

If this afternoon was any indication, it was going to be an all-nighter.

Ryan addressed the group that was gathered in the conference room. "Let's start at the beginning. Steve, you're up."

I raised my hand before he got started. "Can each one of you also update if you have the information about what kind of good deeds they did?"

"Why's that important?" Steve questioned flippantly.

"We think it's part of the pattern. I just got done interviewing some witnesses, and this needs to be added to the list."

"Okay." Steve looked at the detectives gathered in bewilderment.

"Our first person was killed on January 20th. She was brought flowers, and the card is the same as the others. Hit with a long wooden blunt instrument."

Ryan interrupted this time. "The M.E. says it's nun chucks. This is a well-thought-out murder. We're pretty sure that he has nothing personal against these ladies. He might not have even met them."

Steve took the update and continued listing each victim. "We have twelve dead now, all with the same M.O. The only different thing is the type of women he's targeting. The victims could have been rich or poor, it seems to make no difference. They were all committed in daylight, but some of the ladies weren't discovered until a day or two later, making it harder to form a pattern."

"Thank you, Steve. Leslie, can you update us on what's happening in Dallas? For those that don't know, this is a joint task force, and you will treat Leslie with the same respect that you would me. Just because our chiefs had a beef doesn't mean that we can't work together and catch a murderer." He nodded at me to stand in front of the board.

"We have at least seven that have been killed, and there may be a few out there that one of our teams didn't recognize or know about because we're close to the sign of Aquarius being over. This is linked to the zodiac symbol, but we just aren't sure what the message is yet. Most of the victims had few family ties, or their spouses weren't around when they were killed. Each one of ours was philanthropic and working in some way to help effect social change. I believe that's why we had a few people that were on the more wealthy side. They gave to groups that needed their financial help, even if they weren't volunteering personally. Someone has to pay for the services to continue running." I looked at those gathered, and most were paying attention. There were a few that weren't too involved.

"She sounds like that psychic woman that came in raving about good versus evil."

I took a deep breath, trying to ignore what he'd said.

"This man is targeting women who are old enough to be on their own, but he seems to stop before they hit their fifties. I thought when February hit that the murders would stop, but the signs go from the twentieth of each month until the twentieth of the next one. So we're on the twelfth of February. We have eight more days if he sticks to the pattern." I went and sat back down.

"All right. Now I'm going to open the floor to the craziest theories and ideas. If we throw enough at the wall, something might stick." Ryan fixed his gaze on Steve. "Do you have any thoughts about how we might catch this guy?"

Steve sat up from his slumped position and ran a finger over the tip of his nose. "Personally, I think this guy is crazy. He just gets his kicks from taking flowers to women that have wronged him, and he whacks them over the head. I mean, who chooses nun chucks as a weapon?" he scoffed.

"He's too controlled to be a rejected suitor. There's no way someone mad at the victims could only strike one blow as he's doing. He might be crazy, and probably is, but he's in charge of the situation," Ted commented from across the table.

"I suggest we pull up a list of all the birthdates for women that are under fifty in our areas. We could narrow them down by a few things, such as they don't have children and they do good deeds. We can buy a list from an internet site and then double-check their social media pages." Ted followed up his comment with a workable idea.

"Agreed. We're going to split this into two teams. Those that narrow the list down and pass the names onto the other team for them to look them up on social media. I think each of these women at least had their sign listed somewhere for him to find them so easily," Ryan ordered.

"Seriously, a waste of time," Steve grumbled.

"Does anyone else have any reservations about this form of investigation?" Ryan questioned sternly.

The room filled with a chorus of "No, sirs."

"Very well. Go get started. Leslie, you can use my office until I get in there. Steve, please stay behind."

I bit my lip, trying not to smile. I might not know Ryan very well yet, but I was certain that Steve was about to be very uncomfortable for the next little while.

It was a good time to find out if Ford had come up with any information on Noah that would help tie him to these murders.

"Ah, it's the love, detective. I'm afraid that I don't have a lot of news for you. He has been at his job most of the days that these murders have taken place. The one lady that you mentioned happened to have an intimate moment with him, but from what I can tell, it ended amicably." Ford's deep voice sent chills down my arms. How could he be so sexy over the phone?

"Does he have an assistant that's a man, or a best friend that would do anything for him?" I had a sudden thought.

He might not be the one doing the murders, but he could be ordering them.

"The only person I've noticed with him is his driver. They seem to have a very close relationship. I'm not sure that his driver isn't someone his parents have watching him. He's very rich, and they could have hired him as a bodyguard." Ford paused for emphasis. "His best friend isn't allowed in the club anymore because he was too violent. Glen Roberts, I believe. I can text you his information shortly."

"Thank you so much. I appreciate it."

"No problem, doll. I might need you to return the favor one day."

The line disconnected, and he was gone.

He was gone, but he'd left me with a few clues that would allow me to work with what might lead to a suspect.

Time flew by as I gathered information on Noah Preston and his friend Glen Roberts. It wasn't hard to find the name of his driver, Bob Spencer, as well, and I was so busy running them through the system that I didn't hear Ryan come in.

"Did you find something?"

I looked up. "Close the door, please."

He frowned at my request, but did it.

"I've been watching someone that was connected to one of our victims. He's a part of the famous Black Tie Club in Dallas. We interviewed him, but he said he wasn't the boyfriend, but they had sex a few times. Something about him has nagged at me, though, and I've been keeping an eye on him and trying to find out more about him."

"Continue."

"A C.I. was recommended for me to talk to, and he was going to find out some information about Noah and Susan, our victim. Noah seems to have alibis for all or most of the murders. It's almost like he knew about them and made sure that someone knew his whereabouts so he wouldn't be blamed. The thing is, I saw him over here at the apartment next to one of your other victims, so I put a small GPS on his driver's hat."

Ryan's eyes widened in surprise, but he didn't stop me from explaining my crazy idea.

"What if the driver or his friend are the ones doing the killings? He could be disposing of all the extras that could be a problem for him. He's on track to being promoted from Manager to an Executive position in the Urban Energy Company sometime next month. He couldn't take a chance that his alternate lifestyle would come out and ruin his promotion."

I pointed to the screen in front of me. "His bestie, Glen Roberts, was kicked out of the club for his more violent tendencies. He doesn't have the wealthy parents or position that Noah does. He could easily have been paying his friend to do this, and no one would suspect them."

"Okay, I do have one question. Why would he use the zodiac signs and have a body count of at least twenty?"

"I think he's trying to cover all of his indiscretions, or take out those he considers a threat to his future plans. This guy is in his mid-thirties. It wouldn't be that hard to have racked up at least twenty or thirty at his age. These women would be the ones who would show up when he goes to run for office in twenty years and cries that it wasn't consensual."

"Where is his friend at the moment?"

"He lives in the garage apartment of Noah's house." I tried not to jump up and down in my chair.

"Interesting. This would take some proof before we could bring them in because of the amount of backlash from Noah's family. They're certain to put all the blame on Glen."

"Exactly. If he's as good a manipulator as I believe he is, then he's managed to make Glen think they're in it together. How does a shift in surveillance sound?" I hadn't done one of these in a while, and it wasn't fun, but if it caught these guys, then I was all for it.

"I'll make some calls and see if we can coordinate so that you have the jurisdictions and they won't give you any hassle for suggesting it." Ryan picked up his desk phone to start making calls.

"I'm going to run to the ladies' room, but I'll be right back." I closed up my computer and packed my bag, taking it with me. Even though I trusted Ryan, you never knew what could happen, and I didn't like to leave things I was responsible for out of my sight.

A voice drifted to me as I came out of the office. "He's just getting him some and doesn't like that. I don't agree with his 'partner's' ideas. They shut the door, and we all know what that means."

Unsure of what to do, another voice chimed in, "Steve, you're disgusting and mad. He dressed you down for being disrespectful to a fellow officer. If he were to hear you now, you would be on desk detail and working holidays for the next year. I'm not telling him, but if this continues, I'll have to report your attitude about female officers to someone higher than Ryan."

"Don't threaten me, you little..." Steve trailed off as someone else walked by. "You're just as bad as she is, which is why you chicks stick together."

"Steve, just consider yourself warned. I'm tired of it, and just because we both have different equipment than you, doesn't mean that you can voice your thoughts out loud to us."

I stood there, just out of sight, and wanted to cheer, but I knew that I would have to walk past them to reach the bathroom. Taking a deep breath, I kept my eyes in front of me and almost ran to the restroom so that I didn't make contact with either of them.

Washing my hands a few minutes later, a woman walked in and stopped before going into a stall. "Watch yourself around, Steve. He's mad, and he'll be looking for anything to get you and Ryan into trouble. Ryan got promoted before he did, and Steve has been after him ever since. Steve's mouth and views of his co-workers were the reason that I had not promoted yet him."

"Thanks for the heads-up. I'll watch my back." Giving her a tight smile, I dried my hands and walked back out to find Ryan headed in my direction.

My stomach gave a little flop. *Down, girl. He's handsome, but off-limits.* I didn't want to give Steve any more ammunition than I already had.

"They approved it, so we're supposed to meet your partner, Joe, in an hour to fill him in on what's going on." Ryan fell in step with me and walked out of the office, unaware of the hate-filled eyes watching us.

Joe met us at the desk and we all convened in the conference room. I had sent the map of the GPS coordinates to the printer so that we could see where the driver had been over the past few days.

"This is where Urban Energy is located, and this is his home. So all the points in between the two are various stops that they've made. We have no way of knowing if Noah or Glen were in the car with the driver, Bob. Do any of these fit the locations of the murders?"

Joe held up one of the pages next to the larger map.

"The car wasn't at any of these over the past few days. In fact, it didn't even leave the area to go to Ft. Worth." Joe continued to look at the two and compare them.

"Well, crap. I thought it would lead us somewhere."

"At least this rules out the driver for most of it, but if he was at the parking garage and left the car there, then it wouldn't show on the GPS."

"I didn't track his car. I put the tab on his hat, which is the one thing he would wear while doing his job every day. If he wasn't wearing the hat, then we couldn't track his whereabouts."

"I went ahead and acquired warrants for their vehicles. If any of them go to where a delivery van is parked, then we'll have them. It's for any vehicles that are registered or being used by one of the three men." Joe held up three separate papers that were all signed and ready for us to implement.

"Bob, the driver, has already seen me, so it has to be one of you two that puts it on the vehicle."

"I'll do it, and two of you go over and see if you can put the trackers on any vehicles that Glen might be using. We know that Noah should be at work, but Glen could be there, so be careful. You might have to wait a while for him to leave the house.”

I knew that Joe wasn’t particularly thrilled to hang out in-car waiting to follow someone.

“Have there been any murders reported today?” I questioned.

“Not yet, but it doesn’t mean it hasn’t happened, just that no one’s found a body,” Ryan interjected.

“All right. Let’s go so we can catch Glen if he goes straight home,” I urged.

“She’s still so new.” Joe shared a chuckle with Ryan.

“Don’t worry, I’ll keep her safe,” Ryan assured him.

“You break her heart and you’ll have to deal with me, even if I’m retired,” Joe warned.

“Right here, boys.” I waved a hand in front of them. “Joe, that’s sweet of you to want to protect me, but I’ve been doing it on my own for a few years now.”

“Hey, just because you can protect yourself, doesn’t mean that your family can’t help you out.” He winked at me. “Now, go before you run out of energy.”

He didn’t have to say it twice. Even though they teased me about it, I had a lot of extra energy.

• • • • ● • ● • • •

Noah's house was in a highly patrolled community, but we were able to find the alley and what appeared to be an empty house. I ran the address, and when nothing came up, we shut the car off. Sitting in the car was going to make surveillance much harder to do without getting spotted.

"There's not a gate on the back driveway. I'm going to go up there and see if Glen's home." I had a hand on the door when Ryan stopped me.

"Both Noah and the driver know what you look like. If they see you, they'll assume that we're watching them and back off. I'll do it, and I can come up with an explanation if I need to."

Exasperated, I held out the trackers and dropped them into his hand. "You're right. Don't expect it to happen very often."

He grinned. "Yes, ma'am."

A few minutes later, he returned.

"I think he just got home because the engine was hot. Maybe we just got lucky."

I'd gotten a text from Jerome about doing something later, but I had to tell him that I was working.

"That the boyfriend?" Ryan asked curiously.

"Potential one. We've only been on a few dates, but he looks promising."

"Well, it's a hard job with long hours. A lot of relationships don't make it."

"How did you and Shea meet? She seems to have a good head on her shoulders, so I'm just curious how on earth you've managed to keep her?"

"Ha! She seems to like me, but honestly, I agree with you. She's above my pay grade, and I have no idea why she's stuck around this long. We met in college through mutual friends. We hung out, and then one day the friends weren't there, and she didn't run away. I asked her out on a real date before I went into the academy. She knew what she was getting into from the beginning, but we had a lot of friends that had gone the way of the military. They were never home, and at least this way, I'm around."

"About halfway into my probation period, she suggested that we move in together because otherwise, we'd never see each other. I wanted to wait to ask her to get married after I went from patrol to detective, so last year, after I was off probation, she got her ring."

"How on earth did you get to be in charge after only two years as a detective?"

"There were a lot who retired, and I had a few breaks when it came to cases that helped put me in front of the brass making the decisions."

"Hmm. So, no kids yet?" I couldn't believe that they'd been together for years, and not only were they not married, but still had no children.

"Shea would love kids, but she wasn't sure how well they would mix with my job. We wanted to make sure that we were financially stable and in a position to take care of them. She's just gotten established in her job, and it will be a year or two before she could take the time off to have one," Ryan explained.

"Sorry. I know it's none of my business. I'm just nosy."

"No problem. What about you? Why are you just now dating? Where are your kids?" Ryan fired back.

"Oh, I see how it is. I just never found a guy that could stay interested in my brain. Most were just short-term, and without a long-term partner, I just wasn't interested in starting a family. I knew that I wanted to be a cop, and I would have to put in my time before I would be able to do the mom thing. Some people were just made for it, and I'm not sure it's my thing." I shrugged, hoping that he would change the subject.

"Now that Shea and I are engaged, people keep asking when we're going to start a family, and it gets annoying. I know it bothers me, and I'm sure Shea hears it more often than I do."

"People mean well, but it's constant. It's why I don't have many close friends anymore. They all got married and are doing their own thing with kids. I love kids, but it's like we're speaking different languages or something."

"Exactly. I help protect the kids and work to catch killers. It's hard to change out of that mindset and think that everything Nick and Patty do is just amazing. I mean, they walked. Doesn't everyone?" Ryan looked extremely confused.

"Yeah, I can see how that might be a problem. Each set of parents are different, I guess. Learning new things is great, but it's not what I plan to spend my time on right now."

I noticed someone come out, but they were only taking out the trash after dinner. My energy was rapidly going away, and we were going to have to take shifts later sleeping if things kept on like this.

Several hours later, we weren't feeling lucky. Nothing had happened, and there weren't any reports of a dead body being discovered. While that was good, it also meant that we had no idea which direction he was going to go next.

"I think we should call it a night. He's not going anywhere. Either he knows we're out here, or he's done for the night. None of the murders have been at night, and we should get some real sleep before we go driving around all over town tomorrow," Ryan suggested.

Stifling a yawn, I agreed. "A real bed sounds nice. Let's just hope this turns something up and we aren't just chasing our tails."

I turned the key and pulled out. My focus had been on the house in front of us, but not on the white van parked three doors down, hidden by a dumpster. It followed us back to the station.

Chapter 11

We all met early at the station and checked on all the tracking devices, but they didn't give us anything unusual from the overnight reports.

"Could we be on the wrong track with Glen and Noah?" Ryan asked doubtfully.

"How do these three get so much information on these women? It would take weeks, if not months, to stalk them this thoroughly. I mean, if he was dating them, at some point he might have found out some information. This level of stalking would take almost all of his time so that he would know their routines. Even if he only watched for a few days and moved on to the next one, he'd have to check on them again to make sure nothing changed before he committed the murder."

Joe looked at both of us to see if we had answered the question. "We've run both these guys through the system, and there haven't been any real complaints. A few speeding tickets, and a few episodes when they were in school for ballooning the president's office, but other than that, they're clean."

"Either they're psychos who know how to hide it well, or we're looking at the wrong guys. I suggest that we bring them in again and see if they rattle very much. We haven't even talked to Glen yet, and he might know something about Noah that would be helpful." My gut wasn't getting quieter about them, and I was getting worried I might have an obsession of my own.

"I'll have some uniforms pick them up. It might be nice to see what their reactions are if they see each other being questioned." Joe nodded to a few of the extras that had been helping out with this large case.

"We've verified that most all of the women who have been murdered so far were into charitable giving or volunteering somewhere to help those who needed it," Ryan added. "Have you heard anything from the psychic again?"

"You still had someone at her house when I went by, didn't you?" I shook a playful finger at him. "It's okay. You told me to see if I could get more information from people if you weren't around. I took you at your word."

"Did you find out anything that might help us?" Ryan prompted.

"Oh, uh, just that most of her skills are just becoming active. She has good readings on people, and offered to listen in to tell you if a suspect is the right one." I grinned, knowing what his response would be.

"Hell no. We're not going to let some civilian come in and tell us who's guilty and who isn't." He stood up and started pacing.

"Well, to be fair, she was getting her degree in psychology and could shed some light on their character from her real-life skills."

He shot me a dirty look, but Joe grinned. "Hey, why not? If she can get here before they get back with those two, there's no reason that she can't watch the interviews. We've got nothing to lose at this point. Call her."

Ryan glared at both of us. "I need some fresh air." He left the room, muttering to himself.

"I get the feeling this lady gets under his skin more than you do, which is kind of funny." Joe sipped his cold cup of coffee and looked back at the board. "What are we missing?"

An hour later, everyone was in place, and Flora was watching from behind the glass as Ryan, Joe, and I entered the room with Glen.

"Hi, Glen. Did the officers tell you why you're here?" Joe started with the questioning.

"Something about a woman that died, I guess. I don't know why that involves me. I don't even know who she is." The shorter young man folded his arms defensively.

"Well, if you don't know who died, then how do you know that you weren't involved?" Joe pressed forward with his inquiry.

"I didn't kill anyone, so it doesn't matter who it is. I didn't do it. Why would I be a suspect in something like this? I don't have a record. I've never stalked or threatened anyone. So what's this about? I may decide that I want a lawyer."

"Are you asking for a lawyer?" Ryan stepped forward.

"Not yet. When you tell me what I'm being suspected of exactly, then I can decide if I need one." Glen looked at each one of us. "I'm going to guess that you don't have any evidence or I wouldn't be here now, would I?"

"Ignore these two. There have been a group of murders, and we have enough reasonable evidence to suspect your friend, Noah. What we can't figure out is if you're both working on it together, or if it's just his thing?" I smiled to calm him down, but it had the opposite effect.

"You think Noah is killing these women and that I'm involved? Boy, are you guys crazy." He shook his head while laughing at us. "I'm gay. Noah's my best friend because he doesn't care about my sexual preferences. I like women as friends. I could never hurt them, much less kill them. Now, Noah does like to get around, but he's not one of these guys that gets angry or hits on women, either."

"So because you're gay, you couldn't kill women?" Ryan frowned at the suspect's logic.

Glen leaned forward. "Most of the time, when you see someone murdering women, they're getting their kicks off. That wouldn't apply to me. I don't have enough hate or anger to slap one, much less hurt them permanently."

"Noah's never had any complaints in the sex department, and most of the women he dates know it's only a short time thing. If one of them came up dead, he wasn't the one that killed them." Glen grinned at the idea of Noah committing murder.

"One of his recent, or even current, girlfriends, was one of those who were found dead," I added, knowing that even if Glen was involved, we weren't going to get anything from him.

"Look, I'm sorry. His last one, Susan, had gone on a little longer than some of the others because she just wanted a sexual relationship. She was driven, and didn't have time for flowers or phone calls. That would have taken her focus off of whatever she was trying to do with some business deals."

"So you'd met Susan?"

"Yeah. She'd been around for about three months. Noah brought the more trusted women back to the house. Not everyone that wanted to sleep with him had pure intentions and wanted a chance to get some of his money. Susan wasn't like that, so she got the more royal treatment." Glen shrugged like it was a normal thing for girls wanting sex had pure intentions.

"There wasn't anything that would make you think he'd have her killed? Or pay someone to do it for him?"

"You mean like a hit? Oh boy, that's hilarious. Women were just a means to an end, a way to scratch an itch. Noah has been told who he's going to marry for years now. When he turns forty, if he hasn't married her, then he loses all of his inheritance from his grandfather. He's got about three or four more years to play around before that happens. He wouldn't have any reason to have one killed."

"All right, sit tight and we'll be back in a few." Joe motioned us outside. "What do we think about what he said?"

"He's got a point. Most gay men don't go around killing women," Ryan agreed.

"Hey, Flora, what's your take on Glen?" I turned to her as we stood looking at him through the glass.

"He has some issues, and hides behind his sexuality. While I don't think he killed anyone, I think he could still have a part in this." Flora looked uneasy.

"My C.I. did mention that he got kicked out of the elite club for being over the top," I mentioned casually.

"Well, let's see what Noah has to say about all this." Joe led us into the other interrogation room.

"Noah, thank you for agreeing to meet with us again."

"Anything I can do to help? Susan was a wonderful girl." Noah placed his folded hands on the table.

"We're just needing a few more details about your relationship. How did you meet? Did you part amicably?" I leaned in expectantly.

"A mutual friend introduced us and we hit it off. We'd been hanging out for the past month or so. It wasn't serious. We both had different career goals, but at the moment, our schedules fit together. We hadn't parted yet because it was a casual thing. We'd been out a couple of days before you guys showed up to tell me that she was dead." Noah brushed a tear away.

"Thank you so much. We're wondering if you've met any of these other ladies?" I opened the folder with several of the dead girls' pictures and put them in front of him.

He flinched at the morgue pictures, but glanced through them, shaking his head no. "I haven't met any of these ladies, at least not that I know of. I'm sorry I couldn't be of more help to you."

"Would your friend Glen be capable of something like this?" Joe left the folder open as he pointed to the wounds on one of the victims.

"Glen? What does he have to do with this? He's gay," Noah protested.

"It seems like quite a coincidence that these women were killed in the same way that Susan was, and we're just trying to connect the dots. Someone killed them, and it just figures that the same person knew them or had a reason to want them dead," Joe argued. "Just because he's gay, doesn't mean he couldn't have killed them."

"Look, I think this is enough of this type of questioning, and if you need anything else, you can call my lawyer. I'll be retaining one for Glen as well." Noah got up and started for the door. "Just because we're protecting ourselves, doesn't mean that we had anything to do with this."

Ryan opened the door and let him through, as there wasn't anything we could hold him on.

"This sucks," I grumbled. "Now we're back to square one again."

A knock at the window startled us, but we cleared out and joined Flora in the other room.

"Have you seen the paper with the horoscope for this month?" Flora held up a copy of the daily that had been sitting on the table.

"No. What's so exciting about it?" I questioned.

"It predicts the deaths of those born this month." Flora pointed to the daily horoscope.

There will be a new person that arrives with life-changing news on the day of your birth while the sun is in the sky. Beware of strangers who bring death hidden by happiness.

"That's not a proclamation of death," Ryan scoffed, picking up the paper to read it for himself.

"True, but look at yesterday's paper. It's the exact same message. Normally, if you have a daily horoscope in a paper, it will change every day. Look at the other signs. They're different from yesterday to today. Why is Aquarius the exact same?" Flora pulled the two papers together so that we could look at them side by side.

"Could someone change the horoscope to say what they wanted?" Joe seemed leery of the idea.

"The only way to find out is to call the paper and see who was working on it." I turned to go back out to the desk area to make the call.

"Nick, is there any way you could get me the papers for the last few weeks?" I asked as I walked past his desk to mine.

"Sure. Is there a break in the case?"

"We're checking something out, and it might just point us in the right direction," I replied over my shoulder.

Minutes later, we had my desk covered in newspapers while I was on hold for the right person.

"They're all the same, from the twentieth of January through today. The other signs all have different ones for each day." Ryan pointed to the circled words spread across the papers.

"Yes, I was looking for the person in charge of writing your horoscopes? It's for a police investigation, and I need to find out if they are written in-house or from a national databank?" I turned my attention back to the person on the phone.

"Normally, they're written in-house. Carl Sanders is in charge of that, and he's working from home today."

"Do you have a phone number that we can reach him at?" The frown on my face widened as they told me they couldn't give out that information over the phone. "Thank you. Have a great day." I disconnected in frustration.

"Got it. Carl Sanders lives in the Highland area." Nick waved a post-it with an address.

"Let's go." I paused as we left. "Thank you, Flora, for your help. I'll call you if we find out anything important. Nick, can you please see that Glen is released for the moment?"

Joe and Ryan grinned as they waited for me to catch up. "What's so funny?"

"You're already starting to sound like a detective, giving out orders and expecting them to be followed." Joe patted me on the back. "I'm still driving my car over there."

"Thanks, I think. We'll drive over there in Ryan's vehicle that doesn't smell like day-old fries." Hearing praise from my co-workers was nice, but we hadn't caught the killer yet.

Carl Sanders opened his front door after Ryan held up the badge to the peephole. "May I help you, officers?"

"Yes. We have a few questions about your daily horoscope in the paper," Joe began.

"Oh, sure. Come on in and have a seat. I'm working from home today since my daughter wasn't feeling well. What is it that I can help you with?" He took a seat in a chair surrounded by papers, books, and a laptop perched on the ottoman.

"Was there a reason that all the Aquarius horoscopes for the month are the same? Also, do you do the horoscopes for the Ft. Worth papers as well?" I took a seat opposite him on a nice leather couch.

He scratched his head in confusion. "They're not the same? I send in the dailies a week at a time, and I never put the same thing twice. Otherwise, I'd be out of a job."

I laid out several of the past few week's papers. He picked a few up and started reading through each one.

"What on earth is going on?" He threw the papers down and picked up his laptop. "These are the ones I sent in just last week." He turned his email toward us to look at the dates.

"So if you weren't the one doing this, how could that have happened? Is it a glitch in the system?"

"No, it can't be because all the others are correct. You would have to copy and paste each thing into the right section. Why would you do just one month's sign wrong but get the others correct? It just doesn't make sense." He jumped up and started pacing behind the oversized chair.

"Who would have received these from you?"

"The editor, and then copywriters."

"Could someone have made changes? And would they have had to be there in the building to do it, or would there be a way to do it electronically?" If there was a chance that a camera had picked up the killer making these changes, then we might just have a killer.

"Hold on." Carl picked up the phone.

"King, I've got the police at my house, and they're wanting to know why we ran the horoscope section with the same Aquarius prediction all month? I have the emails I sent you. How could they have gotten changed? Hmm, I see. Yeah, I'll let them know." He hung up and walked back to his seat.

"It was a special request. He had a letter on his desk about three days before the month started with the request that he print it all month so that a friend would be sure to see it before their birthday. There was cash along with the request. He didn't think it was a big deal and didn't keep the letter after it went in the system."

"Great, another dead-end." I looked at the other two in frustration. "Thank you, Carl, for your help. If you have anything like this happen again, please give us a call."

"I'm just sorry I couldn't help you more. This is such a weird request, and I'm surprised that my boss didn't mention it before. But I've been out a lot with sick kids. You miss out on things when you're not there daily." He showed us to the door. "I hope you catch who you're looking for."

"This person knew what they were doing when they set all of this up. It's no wonder that we're running around chasing our tails." Ryan kicked at a pebble that was on the sidewalk. "I'm going to head back to my station. If something comes up, let me know, but I need to make sure we're doing everything we can from my end."

With him gone, I was stuck catching a ride back with Joe.

"I'm going to go hang out with the IT guys for a while and see if we can come up with a search that will let us find out who this could be."

"Knock yourself out. When you get done, go home and take a break. If we get a body, they can call us in. The boss will be glad to have us off the clock for a little while." He stopped at the front of the station.

"You're not going to come in?"

"Nope. My mind's overwhelmed, and I need to take a break. I won't be any good if my brain keeps going in the same circles. We need something new to work on with a threat to pull." Joe didn't even turn the engine off.

"Got it. I'll take your advice and head out after I check on this idea." The door closed harder than I'd intended, as Joe wasted no time pulling away.

The tech guys were in their own little department on the bottom floor with the older records. The nerds of the department had gone through the same training and made it through their probationary period until they were transferred directly to the computer area. It was like an entirely different world. They even had their own language.

A few catcalls met me as I walked in the door. I sometimes dabbled with computer tech when I was home and needed something for a hobby. Computers were much easier than getting a cat would have been.

"Mac, remember that request I brought you the other day? Have you had any luck with it?" He didn't even look up as I took a seat next to him.

"Nope. We widened the area, but with only a van to go on, it could take a while." He shrugged.

"Any chance I could take a try at it? I know kind of what we're looking for and when. I'd want a chance to catch this guy."

"Sure, but don't tell the boss that you can work one of these things, or he might put you down here permanently." He grinned and logged in on the computer in front of me.

"Do you know how to run the search software?"

"Yeah. I helped on a case last year and learned how to make it do what I wanted then." I cracked my fingers, ready to get started.

"Have fun." He turned back to his screen to continue working on whatever it was before I'd interrupted.

Time passed quickly, and it was only when Mac stirred I realized I'd been analyzing traffic videos for several hours.

I started to log out so that I could follow Joe's advice and get some rest when Mac stopped me.

"Hey, don't log out. I'll keep running the search for you with the perimeters that you set when I get back from grabbing dinner. It can work while I'm on this other thing, and I'll check on it."

I got up and stretched, moving out of his way.

"Holy cow, woman. When you said that you knew how to run a search, you weren't kidding. If we can't find your guy, then there's nobody else that could do it." Mac looked over at me in admiration.

"The robotics team in college might have been one of the things on my resume. I don't like to flaunt it because then people treat me differently."

"Totally gotcha, girl. Now go, and I'll hit you up if I find something."

He kept shaking his head and staring at the screen in wonder.

Thinking of how people treated me made me think of Jerome. I needed to work off some of my extra stress, and I knew just the thing to do it.

"Laters," I called as I scanned my badge to leave, but Mac never looked up, forgetting dinner in his hurry to work.

Chapter 12

J erome's cottage looked pretty in the setting sun, but there was no way to tell if he was home since he didn't have a car. It had seemed like such a great idea to come over, but now that I was sitting here, I was beginning to feel more like a stalker.

What if our guy had another car that he was using to watch each victim with? He would have had to visit each home in something other than the van so that the neighbors wouldn't be suspicious.

A knock on my window startled me. Jerome was standing at my passenger side door, so I rolled down the window.

"Sorry, I had a free moment. I hope you don't mind that I popped by." Cringing as I waited for his answer, I realized that it had probably been several days since I'd called him. "You probably thought I wasn't ever going to call you again."

"Nope. I've been following things and knew that the birthday killer must be the case you were working on."

Jerome opened the door and got in next to me. "I knew this case was bad, and we had only just started dating. I can't expect you to give up your job or call me every day. If you did, I would be worried that you were a little too clingy. Is everything okay?"

"Yeah...no, not. I'm frustrated that we've worked so hard and this person continues to keep us chasing our tails. Just as soon as we find something that we think will make sense, it's proven that it has no real connection. I have the one who I want to be the suspect, but it appears he has absolutely nothing to do with this," I complained.

He didn't say anything, but placed a hand over mine in comfort or support, I'm not sure which.

"Honestly, I hoped that you would be home and we could pick up where we left off the other day. Then I realized that I would just be using you to get my frustrations out, and that isn't the best way to start a relationship."

"Nonsense. I'm a guy, remember? You can take out those kinds of frustrations on me anytime you want. I'm home, available, and consenting, so why are we sitting in a car?" He grinned at me, waiting for my answer.

"You're not mad that it's been a week with not even a text from me?" This wasn't the kind of reaction I was used to from guys.

"Nope. I had a life before you came around, and while I'd like to see where this goes, I'm not going to wait by the phone for you to call. We're adults, life happens, and that doesn't change just because we might be dating."

"I think you might be the perfect man." I hopped out and walked to his side of the car, opening the door for him. "Care to help me relieve some stress?"

"I'm so not perfect. You'll figure that out pretty quickly, but I would love to help you with that." He took my hand and led me into the house.

The door hadn't even closed all the way when he pulled me into his arms. For once, I didn't hold anything back, or try to overthink things. I let go, and could feel how amazing it was to let someone else do the leading for a change.

Two hours later, a trail of clothes told the story of how much closer we were.

I propped myself up on my elbow. "I don't know about you, but I'm starving. Any chance you've got food in here, or should we order something?"

He got up and walked over to where his pants had landed and fished out his cell phone. "I've got places to eat on speed dial. What are you hungry for?"

"Tacos," I blurted out, suddenly ravenous for some.

"Soft or hard?" He wagged his eyebrows at the extra meaning.

"Soft and loaded. Better order me four, because I could eat a horse right now."

He typed for just a second before looking up. "The PETA people might have an issue with a cop that eats horses."

"Well, as long as you don't tell the papers about it, we should skate right under the radar. Is it okay if I use the shower?"

"Sure, but I can join you if you'd like?"

"Um..." I trailed off.

"You need some alone time? I'll grab you a clean shirt and use the other shower." He moved to the closet to find something for me to wear.

"No, I didn't mean to kick you out of your shower. I'll just..."

He came back and leaned over, turning my face to his. "It's all good. I think you wore out the equipment, anyway. I'm not as young as I used to be, so I can't keep going until I have some food. Neither one of us is around other people in their personal space." He held out a stack of clothes. "Don't be long. The food should be here in just a few minutes." He kissed the tip of my nose and walked out of the room toward the guest bathroom.

Crap, now I felt even more like a heel. He was just too good to be true.

I caught a whiff of lovely smells. I needed to shower just in case something else happened. I couldn't afford to show up looking like I did right now. Showering seemed my best option.

The doorbell rang as I was rinsing the soap out of my hair, so I hurried to get dressed quickly. Reusing my same pants, I'd stuffed my panties in my pocket and decided that commando was better than putting on old ones again. I was going to have to start carrying an extra bag in my car if this became a regular thing.

He rapped on the door. "Food's here, and they delivered a horse with it just for you."

A smile lit my face. "Be right there," I called back.

Raking fingers through my hair would have to do until I could use a comb. I had issues with sharing other people's personal hygiene stuff. That was how things were passed from person to person, and I so did not need that right now.

As I came through the door, Jerome was placing all the food on the coffee table. "I thought we could watch a movie while we ate, and then see if we were up for round two." He looked at me to gauge how I was feeling post-sex.

"Sounds good, unless we get another dead body. But food is the most important thing right now."

He put a comedy on about a woman named Tammy who could be a life coach. We inhaled the tacos and landed on the couch, snuggled together, leaving the trash where it was, which was difficult for me because I liked to have things clean.

Just relax and enjoy it.

The credits were rolling across the screen, and Jerome pulled me around to face him with a gentle kiss on my lips.

The phone rang right then, and we both groaned.

I rolled over and grabbed it as I sat up.

"Yeah?" The clock said it was almost midnight.

"We've got another body."

"I'll be right there."

Jerome was sitting next to me. "Duty calls, huh?"

"Maybe we can do this again in a few days." I scrambled for my boots as I collected my scattered clothing.

"I'll be around. If I have to go out of town, I'll let you know beforehand," he assured me.

A quick kiss and I was gone again.

Why couldn't death be a little more convenient to my sex life? And it had been good. Maybe the best I'd ever had now that I thought about it.

This same scene wasn't any different from the other couple of dozen before it, but this time, the mother had found her daughter.

"I came over when she didn't answer. The first couple of times I tried not to worry, but she'd been planning to come over to get her present. When she didn't show up or answer, I drove over. I live three hours away, but I just got in my car and came," the grief-stricken mother cried as she answered our questions.

"When was she supposed to be at your house?" Joe tried not to glance at the body as the coroner placed the bag over her.

"When she got off work, she was supposed to head out and be at my house at about eight, depending on traffic. She always calls me when she leaves so that I know when to expect her. Normally, she has Fridays and Saturdays off, and we were going to celebrate her birthday tomorrow." She burst into sobs again.

I had walked around while Joe was asking the questions. "It doesn't appear to be any different from the others. I'll go question the neighbors and see if they saw anything."

Not expecting anything different this time, I approached the group of neighbors that were gathered just outside the crime tape. "Did anyone see anything earlier today?"

"Not today, but when are you going to take care of that car that keeps parking outside of my house at all hours of the day and night?" A little elderly woman held tightly onto her small dog.

"Which car? Did you file a report?"

"Of course I filed a report," she responded indignantly. "Several times, but by the time you would get here, it would be gone."

"What color was it?" This might be the break we'd been looking for.

"It was a little blue car, couldn't hold more than two people comfortably. I gave the last officer the license plate number." She patted the little dog. "Are you going to make sure that he doesn't come back? It's having people around that don't belong that causes things like this to happen to nice people."

"Yes, ma'am. I'll pull the reports, and if I need to come back and get the plate number from you again, will that be okay?"

"I suppose so. At least you seem to be interested. None of the others were. They just thought I was a crazy old lady."

"I certainly don't think that, ma'am. We'll do our best to make sure that you aren't bothered again."

I could almost guarantee that the killer wouldn't be back or park in front of her house again.

"It's past my bedtime, and Jessie needs her beauty sleep as well." The older lady walked back to her house.

The others gathered around didn't say much until she was out of hearing range. "She's a crazy old lady. She's always calling the cops or the firemen to come and check out something that she's seen. We've had meetings about her crying wolf, and it was causing trouble for the rest of us."

"Be that as it may, she might have seen something that could give us a lead on our killer. We have to follow up on everything, just in case."

I stayed and asked a few more questions, but nobody seemed to have seen anything, or they were at work during the daytime. Personally, I thought that the old lady might be the only reason they hadn't all been robbed or killed already.

"Joe, I think we might have a break. I'm going to go back to the station and pull some reports."

"Sure, just text me if you find out anything." Joe was still trying to calm the mother down enough that they could get her to a hotel for the rest of the night.

He seemed to have it under control, so I headed back to my car, ready to pull all the reports and have a talk with one of the patrol guys if they had missed something this big.

An hour later, I was still pulling out reports from the neighborhood. Mrs. Henderson had called on multiple occasions about all sorts of things, but the reports of a vehicle had started shortly after Christmas, only lasting a week.

It was a blue car, but the plate number that she'd given me hadn't matched the car's description. It was registered to a warehouse, and said that it was a van, not a car. Our killer must have switched the plates and had been using some he'd gotten from somewhere else.

I went back down to visit Mac, but he'd gotten off at midnight, and the other crew was on duty.

"Ted, do me a favor and run the plates on any vans seen in this area from about noon today until about seven. Pretty please? I think our killer switched the plates from his car to the van he was driving. How long do you think it will be before you have a chance to do that?" I didn't know Ted very well, but was hoping that Mac would have mentioned what we'd been working on only a few hours before.

"Sure, I've got one I'm doing now. I can do your request next, since this is a top priority. It may take a while, though, so I'll email it to you and the other primary on the case. That okay?" Ted hardly even glanced up at me from the counter where you had to sign in.

"If I haven't heard from you when I get to work in the morning, I'll come to check on it." There wasn't much else I could do tonight, and Joe would have to file his reports when he got in since he'd been first on the scene. I'd already put together the reports on my interviews, and I was almost dead on my feet.

I shot Joe a quick text. "Hey, IT is working on a trace. I'm going home. I will work on it if they haven't reported back in the morning. Night."

Joe's response was almost immediate. "Go ahead. I may not get out of here before morning. One of us should get some sleep."

I was almost too numb to care about the bodies that were continuing to pile up. I could only hope that this was going to be the break we needed to find the killer before he murdered again.

Chapter 13

My alarm rang, and I groggily rubbed my eyes, trying to get them open. The calendar on the wall mocked me as I began to clear the fog from my head.

February nineteenth. On the last day of the Aquarius sign, and we had thirty murdered women.

Was the end of the cycle a signal that the murders would stop?

Brushing my teeth, I contemplated my weary face in the mirror. There were circles under my eyes, and my new detective glow had faded. When lives were taken and you hadn't caught the killer, it was hard not to take it personally. I was going to have to learn a better way to cope with the new part of my job.

Dressing slowly, I finally made my way out the door as my phone dinged. It was a text from Joe to me and Ryan.

"Hey, the IT guys sent over the reports you were asking about. Get in here now. I'm only waiting on you and Ryan a short while."

Suddenly, I had energy again. "I'm on my way. Wait for me ☺."

I grabbed my keys and raced out the door, but I realized that I would need some caffeine as well.

A quick pit stop later, and I walked in just seconds before Ryan appeared in the conference room.

Joe grabbed the coffee I'd brought and started explaining without giving us a second to sit down.

"The IT guys sent this to us late last night. I slept here and got an early start. They found a van with a license plate number that has been in the area of several murders. We're putting together a team, and I sent the warrant in to be approved for the house."

"Does it lead back to Noah?" I asked hopefully.

"No, it doesn't." Joe frowned.

"Then who does the plate trace back to?" Ryan asked, just as puzzled as the rest of us.

"It's a work vehicle registered to Urban Energy, but when I checked with them, they said it was last checked out from the warehouse by Ron Black." Joe let the name drop. Everyone went silent.

"Ron Black? We sat there and held his hand while his wife died. How could he be the driver?" My system wanted to go into shock. "We could have prevented all of these other ladies from dying!"

"Is there a warrant on his home?" Ryan laid a hand on my shoulder as I tried to process the information.

"Yes, we were only waiting for both of you. They should have it sent to me by the time we get there." Joe took his cup of coffee and moved to the door.

"Ryan, can you drive us?" He looked at me and I nodded.

I would be fine. It was just going to take a second to process.

By the time we pulled up to his door, I was angry and ready for some answers.

"We're going to approach the door and see if he'll just let us talk to him. Stand down unless I tell you," Joe cautioned the other officers that had parked farther down the street and out of sight.

"How do we explain an extra officer?" I asked, taking a last gulp of coffee.

"You're training me." Ryan grinned. "You have to be plausible while giving yourself away inside."

We approached the house. Ron's car was in the driveway still. I wasn't sure if he'd returned to work after his wife's death. Actually, there were a lot of missing pieces that Joe didn't tell us before we all left, or I'd just zoned out when he said Ron's name.

They let me do the knocking because no matter how much the world wanted everyone to believe that sexism didn't exist, people still felt less threatened by a woman cop than they did by a man.

Letting my anger build was only going to warn him if I knocked on the door as loud as I wanted to. Holding back was difficult, but I did it. When my knuckles touched the door, it swung open just a little bit.

Instinctively, all three of us were reaching for our weapons. "Police, is anyone here?" I called out loudly.

It irked me that I had to warn suspects that I was entering their homes and let them know where I was at.

The three of us spread out, but we only made it to the living room.

Hanging from the railing was a rope that was around Ron's lifeless neck. His neck had snapped, and a note was pinned to his shirt.

"Crap!" I muttered. "I wanted answers."

"We're going to need the coroner." Joe radioed those waiting.

"We'll check the rest of the house." Ryan took off up the stairs, and I swung around through the kitchen.

"Nobody's here!" he called down.

"It's all locked up." I came back to where Joe was standing with the body.

"Ryan, can you reach that letter on his shirt if you stand on a chair?" Joe was looking up at the body that was still a good six feet off the ground.

"Yeah." He pulled on some gloves before he moved a chair over to stand on, barely reaching the paper pinned to the body.

He carefully opened it and started reading out loud.

"I am the birthday killer that you've been looking for all month. There is no real reason except for the fact that my wife had to die, and what better way than on her birthday? Next, you're wondering why did all those other women have to die? Well, Detective, it was all part of the grand design. It's the cycle of life. The balance must be kept, and those who volunteer promise to follow the rules. The consequences are not good for those who don't obey."

"My wife *was* cheating on me. Just not on the day I killed her. My tears were real, but it was that she had to die for her unfaithfulness. The universe sent out its own version of karma, and my death completes the cycle this month, for I must pay for all that I have done."

"Have fun next month, Detectives. Signed, Ron Black."

"Wow. So he planned all these murders to cover up his wife's death? That was a bit overkill, don't you think?" I shook my head in disbelief.

"He could have felt so guilty afterward that he just couldn't handle it, so he killed himself. Many couples don't survive the other's death. He listed each death and its location. That's a confession to me, and at least we can write up our reports and take a few days off." Joe slid the note into an evidence bag.

"That's it? We're just going to take his word for it? It seems to be very convenient to me."

"I sent a few officers out to work things from the warehouse side. I'm betting if we look around a little bit, we'll find something that tells us where he parked the van. It should close things up nicely."

"Why were there two sets of flowers when his wife died if he brought her one set?" I just couldn't let it go. It wasn't adding up in my head yet.

"He probably bought two sets and dropped one on the floor after he murdered her. Or he could have had one set delivered and swapped the cards out himself. I know it's hard to let go, but this is pretty cut and dried. There are no signs of a struggle, so unless the M.E. finds something, then we're stuck, anyway. I'm pretty sure that there won't be any more murders."

Joe's cell rang. "Yeah, you found it? We'll be right there."

"They tracked the van. It's in a storage facility about five miles away."

"All right. Do I need to stay here?" I motioned to the crime scene techs that were taking pictures and lowering the body.

"Not if you want a ride back to the station at some point. Hey, cheer up. It's over," Ryan answered for Joe.

"Great." I pulled my gloves off and put them in the trash can.

• • • • ● • ● • • •

Even an examination of the crime scene didn't make me feel any better, so when Joe sent me home, I knew that I needed to make one more stop before I landed in my bed for the next few days.

Flora was waiting for me when I arrived at her doorstep.

"I've made breakfast. Anything you need to ask can be done over a nice meal, because I'm guessing that you haven't eaten in quite a while." She smiled at me, instantly putting me at ease.

"Thank you." I sank into a chair and felt tears come to my eyes at her kindness. "You didn't have to do all this." The table was set with eggs, toast, jellies, and a steaming cup of chamomile tea.

"You need to be spoiled occasionally. I fear that this month you've been overworked by all that's happened." Flora took a seat across from me, holding out her hands for mine. As soon as they touched, she began, "Blessed be to the creator of our universe. We honor the fact that you have chosen us to stand against those who would bring evil into the world. Thanks for these provisions, and may we use them wisely. Grant us peace." She squeezed my hands and let go.

"Um, Amen? My partners think we've found the killer. He's dead, and a note was attached that told who he murdered each day, including his wife." I took a bite of food, and a small moan slipped out. "This is delicious."

She just smiled and sipped her cup of tea. "You're not feeling that his death clears things up?"

"No. I hate to be beating a dead horse, but I'm certain that this one man had something to do with it. There's no evidence of that, and at this point, everyone is so happy to have a closed case that they aren't going to look any further."

"You think this man was murdered instead of committing evil against himself?"

"Um, if you're saying that he killed himself and so he's cursed, I would have to agree with the cursed part. Yet, it just seems too easy. The guys think it's because I thought he was innocent of his wife's death, and it's my first detective case, so I'm not able to let it go." I sighed as my body gained some energy from the hot food.

"Is that what's bothering you? It's over, and you need something to keep you going?" she probed.

"No, yes. I don't know." I rubbed my temples. My mind was so wound up that it was starting to throb.

"May I make a suggestion?"

"Certainly."

"If you feel comfortable with it, I think you should go lay down on the couch when you're done eating and sleep. Once you've slept, then if you wake up and still feel this way, you'll know that it's not an emotional feeling. The case isn't going to unclose itself while you rest and gain a clear head. What do you say?"

"I think you might be the best friend ever, but are you sure it's not imposing upon you?" The thought of driving home now seemed like a huge problem and wouldn't be wise.

"Absolutely. I have to go to class so you'll have the house to yourself until this evening when my roommate gets home from work. I'll text her so that she won't be surprised when she comes in case you are still here."

"Oh, Flora, you are such an angel."

"Let's get you tucked in. That tea will help offset the coffee. I'm sure that you've been drowning in for the past few weeks and relax your system."

She guided me to the couch and left. I had barely unlaced my shoes when she came back with blankets and a pillow.

My eyes closed on her clearing away the food, and that was the last thing I remembered as I fell into a sleep coma.

• • • ● ● • ● ● • • •

I woke with a start and realized that I wasn't at home. My eyes fell to a note on the coffee table. *Leslie.*

"I didn't want to wake you when I left. Make yourself at home. I brought you the paper. Take a look at the front page."

On the front in large letters, "Birthday Killer Commits Suicide, Story on Page Five."

It gave an accurate portrayal of the events and the number of people that were being attributed to this killer in both cities. There was his picture, and right beside it was his wife's picture. "Man starts killing spree to cover his wife's murder and then regrets it, taking his own life."

February the twentieth would have a new horoscope.

"The eclipse during Aquarius will have drained your energy. It's time to recover and be flirtatious."

Whew! There wasn't anything about death or dying in print, so maybe the others were correct that it was truly over.

I turned the card Flora had left me over and wrote: "You were right, sleep helped my perspective. I'm going to go home and shower. Maybe we can have lunch sometime next week. Thanks, Leslie."

My boots didn't take long to get on, and I opened the front door to step into the bright light. I'd slept for almost twenty-four hours. It was time to let the case be closed. If something happened in the future regarding Noah Preston, I would worry about it then.

With my step much lighter, I was ready to face the world again and maybe take a shower. This had been the longest month on the job I'd ever had. Maybe it was time for a fresh start. Thank goodness Spring was right around the corner.

Want to read more?

Pisces—Book 2 in the Murder of the Zodiacs is available.

A Note from the Author

If you enjoyed this story, please leave a review even if it is one short sentence. Do you want to know when the next book comes out or to get to know me better? Feel free to stalk me on all the social media sites. (No real-life stalking, because that's just not cool.) Thanks for reading and I hope to hear from you.

-Paris Morgan

Also By

More Books from Paris Morgan

Murders of the Zodiac

Aquarius Book 1

Pisces Book 2

Aries Book 3

Taurus Book 4

Gemini Book 5

Cancer Book 6

Leo Book 7

Virgo Book 8

Libra Book 9

Scorpio Book 10

Sagittarius Book 11

Capricorn Book 12

Secrets and Lies

Witness Protection Book 1

Silence Book 2

Hidden Ties Book 3

Cinderella and the Serial Killer

Also Writing as Alathia Morgan:
Against Zombies Series
Moms Against Zombies Book 1
Military Against Zombies Book 2
Co-Eds Against Zombies Book 3
Churches Against Zombies Book 4
Geeks Against Zombies Book 5
Governments Against Zombies Book 6
Farmers Against Zombies Book 7
Freedom Against Zombies Book 8

Dead Cities Series
Dead in Dallas Book 1
Dead in Denver Book 2
Dead in Detroit Book 3

Infected History Series
Infected Waters: A Titanic Disaster Book 1
Infected Poppy Fields:
A WWI Disaster Book 2
Infected Storm Troopers:
A WWII Disaster Book 3
Ghost Ship

Writing Romance as Pepper Paris:

Summers of Love

Carter: Summers of Love 1

Kelly: Summers of Love 2

Wade: Summers of Love 3

Jay: Summers of Love 4

Feathered Protectors Series

Fierce Book 1

Flight Book 2

Flicker Book 3

Monsters Under the Bed

Rescuing Ruby

Athena

About Author

Paris' passion for finding justice for victims came from working with several organizations that help those in need. Gaining knowledge from a police ride-along and her criminal justice class while in college, it brings an authentic flavor to her characters in her Psychological Thrillers and Suspense Novels. When she isn't trying to figure out a way to save her characters from serial killers, she enjoys watching t.v. shows and reading from her TBR list. She also writes spicy, steamy romances under the name Pepper Paris while fighting zombies under the pen name Alathia Morgan.

https://www.facebook.com/Paris-Morgan-Author-104447718401411

https://www.amazon.com/Paris-Morgan/e/B082WP1Y1X

https://www.bookbub.com/profile/paris-morgan

https://www.instagram.com/parismorgan_author/

https://misdirectedtales.com/